GONE IN THE NIGHT

A BURKE AND BLADE MYSTERY THRILLER

MICHAEL LISTER

PULPWOOD PRESS

Copyright © 2024 by Michael Lister

All rights reserved.

No part of this book may be reproduced in any form or by any electronic or mechanical means, including information storage and retrieval systems, without written permission from the author, except for the use of brief quotations in a book review.

Books by Michael Lister

(John Jordan Novels)
Power in the Blood
Blood of the Lamb
Flesh and Blood
(Special Introduction by Margaret Coel)
The Body and the Blood
Double Exposure
Blood Sacrifice
Rivers to Blood
Burnt Offerings
Innocent Blood
(Special Introduction by Michael Connelly)
Separation Anxiety
Blood Money
Blood Moon
Thunder Beach
Blood Cries
A Certain Retribution
Blood Oath
Blood Work
Cold Blood
Blood Betrayal
Blood Shot
Blood Ties
Blood Stone
Blood Trail
Bloodshed
Blue Blood
And the Sea Became Blood
The Blood-Dimmed Tide
Blood and Sand

A John Jordan Christmas
Blood Lure
Blood Pathogen
Beneath a Blood-Red Sky
Out for Blood
What Child is This?

(Jimmy Riley Novels)
The Big Goodbye
The Big Beyond
The Big Hello
The Big Bout
The Big Blast

(Merrick McKnight / Reggie Summers Novels)
Thunder Beach
A Certain Retribution
Blood Oath
Blood Shot

(Remington James Novels)
Double Exposure
(includes intro by Michael Connelly)
Separation Anxiety
Blood Shot

(Sam Michaels / Daniel Davis Novels)
Burnt Offerings
Blood Oath
Cold Blood
Blood Shot

(Love Stories)
Carrie's Gift

(Short Story Collections)
North Florida Noir
Florida Heat Wave
Delta Blues
Another Quiet Night in Desperation

(The Meaning Series)
Meaning Every Moment
The Meaning of Life in Movies
MORE: Do More of What Matters Most and Discover the Life of Your Dreams

For Sunny
You are my Sunshine!

Don't miss a single new release by Michael Lister!

Sign up for new newsletter at www.MichaelLister.com

1

"I thought we didn't do divorce work," I say.

Blade and I are in St. Andrews during the barely contained chaos of Mardi Gras following Christopher Porzingis. The parade has just concluded, but the residual energy remains. The electric atmosphere is that of a kind of moving drunken carnival.

We are enveloped in the discordant cacophony of a noisy crowd—thousands of adults and children, and hundreds of pets—talking, yelling, singing, laughing, crying, barking, surrounded by the desultory sounds of traffic, the breeze blowing in off the bay, the shrieks of gulls, the incessant honking of horns, and the blare of vehicle radios and parade float sound systems.

The small area isn't equipped for this many people, and the density of the frenetic throng makes it difficult to breathe. It's impossible to move in any direction without bumping into someone. And not just people. It's shocking how many of those in attendance thought it'd be a good idea to bring their dogs.

Blade says, "Your ass knows as well as mine we do whatever

kind of work we can get. Grateful as fuck to get it. But . . . this ain't exactly divorce work."

"It's not? Then what is it, exactly?"

Porzingis is on the opposite side of Beck Avenue. He's a tall, thin, man with dark, closely cropped hair and a neatly manicured stubble beard. He's wearing a retro leather jacket and mirrored shades, and looks like a dark, elongated iteration of George Michael from around the time the "Faith" album dropped.

"More like child custody work."

"I don't like it," I say.

"Ain't got to," she says. "Just got to do it."

Christopher Porzingis, a thirty-something attorney, is in a toxic and vitriolic divorce and child custody dispute with our client. Actually, our client is the law firm where our offices are located. From time to time as part of our rent we have to do investigative work for the firm. This is one of those times.

Porzingis, who has been standing in front of the old Shrimp Boat restaurant, begins to move, making his way down Beck in the direction of Oaks by the Bay.

We follow, weaving in and out of beaded revelers in varying degrees of intoxication, a smear of green and gold and purple swirling around us. One in three people we encounter have faces partially hidden by Mardi Gras masks and at least one hand gripping an open container sloshing out libation onto the street.

Now that the parade is over a mass exodus is underway, and we, like Porzingis on the opposite side of the street, are swimming against the stream of those who are now trekking back to their vehicles.

Like Porzingis, Blade nor I are dressed for Mardi Gras. Blade is in a pair of black ninja webbing drop-crotch multi-strap cargo pants, matte black greasy leather boots, and a black retro leather biker jacket with lots of silver-toned zippers. I'm in jeans and a somewhat wrinkled button-down. Unlike Porzingis, we don't have any beads dangling around our necks.

Unlikely partners, improbable investigators, unconditionally and unquantifiably family, I'm a twenty-five-year-old straight white man who has been told he looks a bit like a young Paul McCartney, she's a twenty-six-year-old gay black woman who looks like a mashup of Black Panther and Storm.

I glance across the street at Porzingis who has paused to look at a kayak in front of Sunjammers, and notice he's alone.

"Where's his kid?"

"Left her with his mother?"

"Wait. Whatever risky behaviors we're here to observe him doing . . . he doesn't do while he has his kid?"

"He has his kid. It's his weekend. And instead of spending time with her, he's down here lookin' to get laid."

"But he left his kid with her grandmother, so she's good, so he's being responsible."

"Look—"

"And who this dude fucks shouldn't have anything to do with how much he gets to see his kid."

"*Who* he fucks don't," she says. "*How* he fucks and *when* and *where* he fucks do."

"*How* he fucks is what I mean," I say.

"Ain't like that," she says. "Got nothing to do with him preferring dick. It's about reckless and even dangerous behaviors. Gettin' fucked up on coke or meth and poppers . . . and he's got this thing for strangers in public places. That kind of shit. It's about how he puts his kid at risk. You know good and goddamn well I wouldn't use someone's sexual orientation against them. As the resident gay in our agency my ass is more invested in protecting people's sexual orientation than yours does—or at least as much."

I shoot her a look

"The hell that look mean?" she says.

"You've always seemed . . ."

"Seemed what, bitch? Spit it out?"

"When it comes to our cases . . . you've always seemed pretty much more or less . . . amoral."

"Pretty much . . . more or less . . . sure you don't want to qualify that shit some more?"

"Just tryin' to ease the emotional blow."

"You know I got even less emotions than morals."

I'm mostly positive Blade is not a sociopath, but her feelings like her conscience, are buried deep beneath the fibrous scar tissue of her heart.

Porzingis is on the move again and we're following, down past Burganbarrel, Janie's Art Fence, and the St. Andrews Bodega.

He turns right at the Native Spirit Museum and Gallery and heads west toward the marina and the vendors lined up along the pier.

As we pass the kids' area of bouncy castles and games I wish I was here with Alana, my five-year-old niece, enjoying her enjoying the fun event instead of following a father who didn't bring his daughter.

The long L-shaped pier surrounding the marina is filled with event vendors in tents, food trucks, and trailers.

We pass between a Tarot reader caravan on one side and a funnel cake trailer on the other.

We are greeted with an olfactory casserole of competing and conflicting odors. The sweet, sugary smell of cotton candy collides with the tangy brine of the bay blowing in on the breeze. The thick, greasy odor of deep fried food mixes with the acrid aroma of stale beer and cigarette smoke and the occasional, pungent stench of pot.

Though a large part of the crowd left following the parade, there's still an enormous mob meandering down the pier, weaving around each other and in and out of the booths of the street merchants.

Many of those operating less busy booths stand out in front of them attempting to entice passerbys to sample their wares like carnival barkers at a circus sideshow attraction.

At the elbow of the L-shaped pier a Zydeco band is playing an energetic rendition of "Paper in My Shoe" by Boozoo Chavis.

Porzingis stands at the back of the crowd gathered to listen to the band. He towers over everyone around him and something about the lascivious way he stands and scans the crowd communicates he's on the make.

We stay far enough back so he doesn't see us.

"All this street food smells good," Blade says. "Got me hungry."

"One of us can grab grub while the other keeps an eye on Tall George over there," I say. "We'd look less conspicuous if we were shoving shitty street food into our faces."

"True," she says. "Plus . . . Lewinsky, Clemons, Bradley, and Sykes will pick up the tab for it."

"What sounds good?"

Before she can answer, Porzingis is on the move again.

He makes the turn and continues down the backside where even more food trucks are set up. Only now he has a companion—a young, short, extremely thin guy with too few tight-fitting clothes.

Blade pulls out her phone and videos the two men making their way toward the bank of portable toilets at the end of the line of food trucks.

"Ah, hell nah," Blade says. "Tell me they ain't about to hook up in one of those nasty ass porta pottys."

"Nowhere else down there—unless they climb into the back of the cop car."

At various locations throughout St. Andrews cruisers with their lights flashing are parked to emphasize the police presence—and there's an empty one parked at an angle just beyond the portable toilets where the official Mardi Gras festivities end.

There are sixteen portable toilets, eight blue and eight pink lined up back to back in two rows. The blue ones face us and the pink ones are behind them facing the opposite direction.

Porzingis and his newly acquired companion walk around the blue ones to the pink ones in the back.

We follow.

There are very few people on the backside of the bank of toilets that form a barrier of privacy from the prying eyes of the other Mardi Grasers.

Blade and I walk past them and continue on to a spot along the railing as if we're here to watch the sunset over the bay.

The little guy enters the last toilet on the end closest to the water and doesn't lock it. Porzingis waits a few moments and when no one is around quickly steps into the same toilet and closes the door behind him.

Appearing to be capturing the sunset, Blade has her camera reversed and records everything the little guy and Porzingis have just done.

"Is that enough?" I ask. "Can we go?"

"Still got to get them in flagrante delicto."

"No," I say. "No way. Come on. That's not necessary."

She approaches the pink porta potty, continuing to video, holding her phone out in front of her sideways to capture everything in landscape mode.

When she reaches the unit, she slings open the door and stands there capturing the undignified porta potty sex.

When Porzingis realizes they are being observed, he stops copulating and pulls up his pants, but the little guy isn't aware of what's going on yet.

"The fuck you doin?" Porzingis says, then frowns and nods as if something has dawned on him. "My ex."

The little guy turns to see what's going on, his huge horse dick dangling down between his legs.

"*Ga-awd—damn*," Blade exclaims. "Is that real?"

I say, "He's obviously a shower."

"*And* a grower, bitch," he says.

Without pulling up his pants he takes a step toward Blade.

"Keep that thing away from me," she says.

Lunging toward her, he tackles her to the ground.

She shrieks like a school girl and says "Burke, get over here and get that donkey dick off me. Now."

On top of her, the little guy pulls out a large knife from somewhere.

I run toward them.

"The hell that come from?" Blade says. "Your ass?"

"Erase that footage right now," he says.

"Okay, okay," Blade says, her voice full of faux panic and fear.

She then bucks him off of her, twists and spins and suddenly they've reversed positions, his knife clattering away on the concrete as she knocks it loose. He's now flat on his back on the concrete and she's astride him. She quickly scoots forward away from his dick, having to sit on his chest to avoid it. From somewhere in the back of her pants she pulls out a much larger knife than the one he had a few moments before.

She says, "I know you want me to say, but I'm not going to."

"Say what?" he says with genuine panic and fear in his voice.

"*You know*," she says. "But I'm not gonna say it. Okay? It's too obvious, too on the nose. You know? So don't press me."

He glances up at me in confusion.

In my best Australian accent I say, "She's not gonna say, 'That's not a knife. *This* is a knife.'"

He looks no less confused.

Blade climbs off him, pockets her phone, returns her knife

to its concealed location, and says, "Pull up your damn pants, man."

We both offer a hand to help the little guy up but he refuses.

Porzingis steps over and pulls him up.

We all stand there for a moment without saying anything, the little guy still not pulling his pants up.

Blade says, "Dude, put your fuckin' dick up. Now. Then get your knife and put it up too. You do anything else and your shitty day'll get a hell of a lot shittier."

"All y'all are doin'," Porzingis says, "is helping a controlling, conniving, wounded woman keep my daughter from me."

"Actually," Blade says, "you the one doin' that. And doin' a damn fine job of it too."

The little guy pulls his pants up, grabs his knife, and quickly walks away, disappearing around the bank of portable toilets.

"And call Guinness," Blade yells after him. "I'm no expert but I think you have a record."

Looking at Porzingis and thinking of his little girl I can't help but think of Alana.

I say, "You know who's keepin' you away from your daughter at this very moment? You. She could be here with you now or you could be at home with her, but you—"

"What? I can't have a little me time?"

"You get her every other weekend," I say. "That's like thirteen percent of each month."

"*Da-um*," Blade says. "Check out the big math skills on Burke."

"Have your *me time* during the other eighty-seven," I say. "And this shit you're doin' . . . it's . . . there's a reason why you're doin' it this way—the drugs, the strangers, the public places—and none of them good. Got nothin' to do with sex and everything to do with trauma. It's compulsive and dangerous and you're not in control. We've all got issues. My main one is anger and goin' to meetings is helpin' me more than I can say."

"Plus," Blade says to Porzingis, "they anonymous . . . which got to appeal to your Grinder ass."

"Think about all you've lost—how many jobs, how many opportunities, how many relationships. Do you want to lose your daughter too?"

Blade looks back at me. "This public service announcement gonna end anytime soon?"

"If you ever want to go to a meeting," I say, "I'd be happy to go with you."

"The hell kinda PIs are y'all?" Porzingis says.

"Wonderin' that myself," Blade says. "Wonderin' that very same shit myself."

2

"I deserve something better than street food after encountering that big ass donkey dick," Blade says.

We are walking back toward Beck, the smoke from the food trucks and the setting sun making the scene look like a movie set.

"But for real," she says. "How can a guy that little have a dick that big?"

"Probably just looked that big because he was so little."

"Sure," she says, her voice thick with sarcasm. "Keep tellin' yourself that motion-of-the-ocean boy."

"I'm gonna text Ashlyn to see if they can come meet us so Alana can play on the jumpy stuff," I say, pulling out my phone and pausing to send the text. "What sounds good to you?"

"I could go for a Pepper JAQ Melt."

We continue up to Beck, around Thai Basil and down to the St. Andrews Bodega for a couple of their pepper jack patty melts.

"I agree with the little guy," I say.

"That he a shower and a grower?"

"We should lose the footage of them."

She shakes her head—more in disbelief and disappointment than refusal.

"We keep the case open," I add. "Follow Porzingis some more. See if this was a wakeup call for him."

"You're unbelievable," she says. "It'd be sweet if it wasn't so scary. People don't change. He's not gonna change."

"Some people change," I say. "I realize it's not many. But some do."

She shakes her head some more. "So young and so naive."

As we reach the bodega and start to enter, we bump into Scotty Walsh, who is exiting.

Beneath his thick, bushy black hair, his big blue eyes widen and his face lights up when he first sees us, but a moment later his eyes become hooded, his open face guarded and wary as he awaits our reaction to seeing him.

He was once our little foster brother and our friend, but he hasn't been either in a very long time now.

An awkward, silent moment passes between us before I say, "Hey, Scotty," and step forward and hug him.

As we embrace I can feel the tension seeping out of his body.

"Hey, Burke," he says. "How are you?"

As I release him and step back, he glances nervously over at Blade.

Blade nods and extends her fist, which he promptly bumps.

"I'm really glad I bumped into y'all," he says. "I've been tryin' to work up my nerve to come see y'all."

I nod.

"Can we talk sometime?" he says.

"How about now?" Blade says. "You talk and we'll eat."

He nods. "Yeah, okay."

He turns and we follow him into the restaurant.

After several years of being in the system, of being shuffled around between children's homes and toxic foster homes, Blade and I were taken in by the Walsh family, a genuinely good and loving family, who treated us like their own.

The Walshes consisted of Benjamin and Kay, an attorney and an architect and their two children Kaylee, who was about six years older than us and Scotty, who was a few years younger.

And for a little while it seemed our days of crappy children's homes and the Russian roulette of foster care situations were over for good.

But our fate changed when Kaylee, who Blade and I had come to love as our own cool older sister, vanished off the face of the earth in inexplicable circumstances.

Kaylee was a junior at the University of Florida in Gainesville when, for reasons no one has yet discovered, she lied to her professors about a family emergency and left campus without telling anyone. Later that night, on a flat stretch of rural road in Georgia, she ran off the highway into a ditch. Then, even with witnesses watching from a nearby farmhouse, in the span of some six minutes, she disappeared without a trace.

The loss of Kaylee meant that the Walshes no longer had anything to give to us and we went back into the system. We were devastated. For a too brief time we had what we most needed, and then it was snatched back from us, and for the rest of our childhoods we knew what was possible, had actually experienced it, but had to exist without it. Of all the horrible things we experienced, it was in some ways perhaps the most difficult.

Scotty leads us to a table in the back and we take a seat. As usual, Blade and I sit facing the entrance.

The St. Andrews Bodega is a deli, butcher, and wine shop,

and smells strongly of the herbs and spices used in its delicacies.

The front door is propped open and the sights and sounds of Mardi Gras continue to drift by and periodically come in.

When the waitress sees Scotty she says, "It was so good you had to come right back?"

"Something like that. Whatever they want is on me."

Blade shakes her head. Still hurt, still feeling rejected and abandoned by the Walshes, still full of resentment, she's unwilling to take anything from them. "We got ours," she says.

We each order the Pepper JAQ Melt, which is chorizo and ground beef smash patties, pepper jack cheese, Thomasville Tomme, and chive aioli.

Scotty orders a glass of red wine.

When the waitress leaves the table, he says, "I wish you'd let me get your dinner."

"We on a case," Blade says. "Client's gettin' our dinner tonight."

"We appreciate it though," I say. "Thank you."

"I've followed your career," he says. "Y'all have been doing amazing work, gettin' some high profile cases. I'm so . . . proud of y'all."

He doesn't mean it to be condescending, but it comes out that way.

Blade bristles.

"I didn't mean that to sound . . . I just meant I'm proud to know you."

"We know," I say. "Thanks, man."

"I . . ." he says, then stops as the waitress returns with our drinks.

"Cheers," he says, holding his glass up but not waiting for us to clink our glasses.

He then leans his head back, tilts his glass up, and drinks most of his wine in one long gulp.

"Damn," Blade says. "It's not a shot."

"I need it for . . . for what I'm about to say. I want you both to know how sorry our family is for what happened."

"For what happened?" Blade asks.

She's not going to make this easy on him.

"After we lost . . . After Kaylee went missing."

"You mean takin' our asses back to the pound?" she says.

"That's not—"

He pauses and downs the rest of his wine.

"I'm . . . Is that what it felt like? I'm so sorry. We were . . . what happened to Kaylee broke us. We're still broken. We were . . . There's no excuse for what we did."

"You didn't do anything," I say. "You were a kid like us. But we understand. It was . . . We get how—"

"We lost her too," Blade says.

"Mom and Dad feel so ashamed," he says. "Losing Kaylee like that gutted them and they feel so much guilt on top of it."

"We to blame for their guilt?" Blade says.

"No, of course not. That's not what I'm sayin'. Not at all. I just wanted to say how sorry we are. That's all."

Our food arrives and Scotty orders another glass of wine.

A constant procession of intoxicated Mardi Grasers stumble into the Bodega, comment loudly on how good it smells, then stumble back out again.

"Tell us about you," I say. "You in school?"

He nods. "I'm at FSU PC. Wanted to go away for school . . . but . . . with what happened to Kaylee . . . Mom and Dad didn't want . . . I just couldn't do that to them. I went to Gulf Coast the first two years and now I'm still at FSU."

"What're you studying?" I ask.

"Was limited in what I could do here . . . I'm finishing up an MS in Civil and Environmental Engineering."

I nod. "That's great."

"What about y'all?" he says.

Blade says, "I'm workin' on an MF in Criminal and Environmental Thugology at LIFE PC."

"I meant besides what I read about y'all and see on the news."

"You knew Burke went to prison, didn't you?" Blade says.

"No. Really?"

When I got popped for aggravated battery, which is a felony, the judge looked at my rap sheet and saw a history of violence —a series of assaults and simple batteries, mostly fights, all of which carried misdemeanor charges. But because there were so many, because my sentencing score sheet was so high, he sentenced me to a year and a day of state prison time and two years of probation.

"He's got anger issues," Blade says. "Or he did until he started attending meetings—least that's what he told Porta Potty Fuck Toilet Boy.

"Wait. Who?"

"He's still on probation," she continues. "Burke. Not Porta Potty Fuck Toilet Boy. Although, he probably should be. Burke even got involved with his probation officer, which is a big ass no-no. But they're not together anymore. She was murdered by a Russian mobster tryin' to kill us."

Lexi Miller, my former probation officer who I was having an affair with, was kidnapped by an unhinged Russian mobster named Dimitri and shot as we tried to rescue her.

He looks shocked and at a loss for words, which is what she was going for. His wine arrives and he guzzles it again. "Ah, man. I'm ... I'm so sorry to hear that."

"Thanks."

I'm still grieving the loss of Lexi and Blade's insensitivity and use of it to mess with Scotty is hurtful.

"I'm still gay," Blade says. "The conversion therapy the creepy preacher put me through after y'all took me back to the pound didn't take. Still partial to pussy. So that about catches you up on us."

"Things are going okay," I say. "Our agency is doing pretty well. We have a family of sorts—including a five-year-old niece who's more like a daughter."

"That's good," he says. "That's real good."

We are quiet a moment, eating and drinking. Every time Blade takes a bite, chewing instead of talking Scotty looks relieved.

"Have y'all kept up with Kaylee's case? It's . . . crazy how much . . . It's got a life of its own. All the podcasts and YouTube videos and SubReddits and shit. The true crime community is insane about it. And now there's gonna be a TV show. Has the producer contacted y'all?"

"Karen McKeithen?" I say. "Yeah."

"Y'all gonna be involved?"

"Not sure yet," I say.

"They claim they're going to break the case and finally let us know what happened."

"Sounds like some shit a Karen would say," Blade says.

"I wanted to . . ." Scotty begins. "I was wondering . . . Y'all have gotten so good at what you do. I was wondering . . . if we might could hire you to find Kaylee?"

"Oh, we gonna find her," Blade says. "We been workin' her case almost since she vanished. No one has ever paid us to find her and no one ever will. We do it because for a little while she was our sister. She was very good to us. What happened to her is why we do what we do. It's about love and justice, not money."

"I didn't mean to . . . Sorry if I offended you."

"You didn't," I say.

"Speak for yourself," Blade says. "I'm offended as fuck. Wanna treat us like the hired help."

"No," Scotty says. "That's not at all what I—"

Blade stands up, tosses a wad of cash on the table and walks out.

"I'm sorry," Scotty says. "I didn't mean to—"

"She's just still raw," I say. "You didn't do anything. It was good to see you, Scotty."

"I actually go by Scott these days."

3

I catch up to Blade in front of Janie's Fence.

"I'm 'bout good and goddanm tired of you," she says.

I feel attacked and want to respond in kind and come to my own defense, but I take a deep breath and let it out slowly.

There are still a few people around, but not many. Most are over on the pier where the vendors and music is.

Beyond the fence and the buildings on Beck, the last of the sun is sinking into St. Andrew Bay, and the twilight atmosphere has an airy, hushed, calm quality to it. It's growing dim, but the art placed on the fence by Floripolis can still be seen.

"You always lettin' everybody off the hook. Always actin' like everybody's friend. You too damn nice and it's wearin' thin."

I wonder if this is as general as she's saying or it's really about how seeing Scotty and being reminded of Kaylee and the Walshes and all we had and all we lost has triggered her.

"You thought I was too nice to Scotty?"

"To everybody . . . Scotty . . . Toilet Fuck Boy. Everybody. You always feel like you gotta be so damn nice. It's like I got a big pussy for a partner."

"Seems like your muff-diving ass would love that."

She tries but is unable to suppress a smile. "Muff-diving?"

"I was trying to be mean for you."

"By using some phrase from the seventies?"

"I don't feel like I'm nice to everyone or try to be everyone's friend?" I say.

"Well, I do."

"I know. And maybe you're right. I may be too nice. Maybe . . . given all we've been through . . . I want to be liked . . . and . . . accepted. But . . . Scotty was thirteen when Kaylee went missing. He lost his sister and—"

"So did we."

She's right. We did. And there's no way to quantify the damage it did to us, but . . .

"We lost a foster sister we knew for a couple of years—and she was away in college most of that time. He lost his only sister of thirteen years."

"Still."

"You can't blame him for what his parents did or didn't do where we're concerned."

"He was speaking for them, wasn't he?"

I shake my head. "He was apologizing for all of them, trying to explain. He felt bad."

"Not bad enough to reach out to us over the past decade."

"He was a kid."

"So were we."

"How much have we reached out to him?"

She starts to say something but stops.

"I get what you're feeling—the loss and pain and rejection. It's all . . . I feel the same things. But Scotty's not to blame. It's not on him. And even if you blame Ben and Kay . . . Think about what they went through—are still going through. The whole thing is fucked. If we're going to blame anyone it's whoever's behind what happened to Kaylee."

"Well, let's find the fuck so I can show him just how much I blame him."

4

"This is great," Ashlynn says. "Thanks for letting me know about it."

We are in the kids' section on Bay View, which is closed for the event.

As the name suggests, Bay View runs along the bay, from the old Shrimp Boat building to the entrance to the marina next to the mammoth Harbour Village condominium complex rising some eight stories where the Harbor House restaurant used to be.

Out over the dark waters of the bay a low slung nearly full moon glows a pale shade of orange like a porcelain bowl of melting sherbet.

Ashlyn and I are standing next to one of the four commercial bouncy houses, a huge red, blue, and yellow castle with climbing walls, slides, tunnels, and basketball goals.

Blade is several feet away, standing on the curb on her phone.

Farther down Bay View, in front of Alice's, carnival and county fair type games line the entrance to the marina pier.

"So glad y'all were able to join us," I say. "I knew she would love this."

Through the mesh, we can see Alana jumping in the main area in her socked feet with several other kids, the Nerf basketballs bouncing around like the small, brightly colored balls in a toddler Corn Popper push toy.

Ashlynn is one of our foster sisters we grew up in the system with. She and Alana live with us. As close as we are, I'm far closer to Alana, who over time is becoming more like a daughter than a niece to me.

"I'm happy to watch her if you want to look around, grab some food, or listen to the zydeco band," I say.

"Thanks," she says. "I probably will."

"Take your time. Enjoy. I'll keep a close eye on Alana."

"Of that I have no doubt. You take better care of her than I do."

Ashlynn calls Alana over and speaks to her through the mesh. "Mama's gonna go grab some food. Are you hungry?"

"No."

"No, ma'am."

"No, ma'am. I'm not."

"Uncle Luc's gonna stay with you. Do what he says."

"Yes, ma'am."

"Love you. I'll be back in a little while."

"Love you, bye."

As Ashlynn walks away I ask Alana, "You ready to try some of the other bouncy houses or play some of the games?"

"No. I want to stay here."

"Okay. Have fun. Be careful."

As she bounces away I can't help but smile.

She is the single source of pure joy in my life.

I glance back at Blade. She's still on her phone.

Unbidden, I think of Lexi Miller, memories of her overwhelming my senses.

The sights and sounds and smells of Bay View vanish and all I can see is her petite, athletic, runner's body in bed next to me, her straight blond hair in a ponytail, the tips of which are damp, and her mesmerizing Gulf-green eyes and the gaze she would fix on me with them. She was strong and tough and sweet and cute and fun and funny. We had some great times together, and I miss her far more than I thought I would.

We weren't together long, didn't have a ton of time together, and, in fact, being together was against all the rules. I was an ex-offender on probation and she was my probation officer. Our relationship could've cost me my freedom and her her job, but our attempts at resistance proved futile in the face of our attraction and desire.

I don't know if our relationship would have lasted. We were on a sort of hiatus when she was shot. But now I'll never know. I not only miss her and still want her, but I feel guilty for what happened to her. In many ways it's my fault.

"Watch this, Luc," Alana says.

My attention returns to the present and through the mesh I watch Alana do a somersault.

"That's so good, girl. Nice job."

"Watch this."

She jumps and spins and falls and bounces back up.

I clap enthusiastically. "Wow. That was spectacular."

I turn toward Blade.

"Did you see that, Aunt Blade?"

She pockets her phone and steps over next to me.

"Do it again, baby," she says. "I missed it."

Alana does another bouncing spinning flopping trick.

"Nice," Blade says. "You got some moves, girl."

"Come back over this way a little, okay?" I say, trying to get her away from some of the bigger kids.

She bounces over toward us.

Blade lowers her voice and says to me, "Sorry I was such a cunt."

"Sorry I was such a pussy," I say.

"Because of how I . . . behaved . . . I'm gonna delete the footage and give Stretch George Michael another chance."

"Thank you. I really appreciate it."

"Maybe for his daughter he'll . . . Nah. No way. Can't even say it."

"Luc," Alana calls from inside the bouncy castle. "Can I have some funnel cake and cotton candy?"

She makes her way over to the mesh wall and stands directly in front of us.

"How about we get one or the other?" I say. "Both would be too much and would probably make you sick. And why don't we get some dinner first? What have you eaten today?"

She shrugs. "I don't know."

"Want to see if we can find some chicken nuggets?"

She give a little shrug again. "I just want cotton candy."

"Come on. Let's get your shoes on and see what we can find."

She half walks half bounces over to the slide and does a belly flop onto the bright yellow plastic. By the time she arrives at the bottom of the slide I am waiting there with her shoes.

Even though it's a cool evening getting cooler her shoes are sandals so she can wiggle her toes. She hates having her toes trapped and immobile.

Beneath the bangs of her messy dark brown hair she looks up at me with her huge dark brown eyes with such pure sweet innocence I want to buy her all the cotton candy and funnel cakes they have.

"There are a lot of people here," I say. "We've got to stay close. Do you want to hold hands or do you want me to carry you?"

"Walk."

I take her little hand in mine and we join Blade who is waiting for us just outside the kids' area and we continue on toward the pier and the vendors set up there.

The cool night lit by carnival lights is accompanied by zydeco music, generators, the frying and grilling of food, and the noise of the crowd, all before the backdrop of the moonlit bay, has the electric feel of celebration and excitement, as if a night circus.

When we reach Moonlight Mystic's small wooden gypsy caravan, Alana asks if she can go inside.

The Tarot reader seated in front of it at an empty table overhears her and says, "Sure. Take her in. Take a picture."

"Can I take a picture with you?" Alana asks. "You're beautiful."

"Of course. You're so sweet and beautiful yourself."

The inside of the small caravan is curtained and beaded and lit by small, multi-colored string lights. Beneath large hanging decorative Tarot cards and a sequined metal all seeing eye, a blanketed couch sits against the back wall.

After the two of them are seated on the couch, Blade and I both pull out our phones and begin to snap pictures.

Alana looks up at the Tarot reader with awe and admiration.

"Okay," I say, "look this way and—"

Suddenly, the barrel of a pistol is pressed to the back of my head.

I glance over at Blade and see the same thing is happening to her.

"Give me your fuckin' phone, now."

Blade says to me, "Have to admit . . . you were right about people changing. When I'm wrong I'm wrong and I admit it."

Moonlight Mystic hugs Alana to herself and leans in front of her.

"Everything's going to be okay," I say to Alana. "Just sit still there and let that beautiful gypsy princess hold you. Okay?"

"Okay," her small voice comes from somewhere beneath her downturned head behind the Tarot reader.

"I'm pretty sure it's the little guy," I say.

"Is it?" Blade says. "Well, how I know that's a gun pressed to my head and not his dick?"

"Refuse to hand over your phone and you'll find out," he says.

"You by yourself?" Blade asks.

"Yeah, so? I can still—"

"You brought two guns?" she says.

"Yeah. One for each of you."

"Where's your tall—"

"Got no time for chitchat," he says. "Hand over the phone and I'm gone."

"I deleted the footage," Blade says. "It's gone. Just like you need to be."

"She did," I say. "Don't ruin the rest of your life over this. Put your weapons up and walk away."

"Not without the butch's phone."

"I just upgraded," she says. "Really don't want to give it up."

"Think about it," I say. "Whatever you think will happen if that footage gets out can't compare with pulling a gun on—"

"Two guns," Blade says.

"Pulling or God forbid using two guns on us. There are so many children around—one of whom means everything to us. Please don't do this."

"Last chance," he says. "Give me the phone or I shot y'all and take it.'

"Okay, okay," I say. "Give him your phone."

"A'ight," Blade says. "I'm going to hand it to you very slowly. Don't shoot me. And I'd like to get it back once you see I already deleted the footage. Okay. Here we go. On three. I'm going to slowly turn and hand you my phone. One . . . two . . . three."

We both turn quickly and grab the guns and knock him to the ground.

I toss my gun to Blade as I jump down on the little guy. Getting caught with it would send me back to prison, and I'm sure we're attracting some attention by now.

At first he struggles but then gives up and begins to cry.

"They ain't even loaded," Blade says.

"Did you really delete the footage?" he asks.

"Yeah, for this fool here. Did the tall dude really not have anything to do with this?"

"Yeah. I'll never see him again. Don't even know his name. Will you please let me go?"

"Empty or not you threaten us with a gun," she says.

"Two of them," I say. "And with our niece with us."

"I'm gonna let you go," Blade says, "but know this you come at us again and I'll kill you. No matter what. No questions. Just lights out. Your swinging dick will swing no more. Understand?"

"I do. You'll never see me again."

I let him up and he runs away, disappearing into the crowd.

As Blade steps over to the railing and drops the guns into the marina, I duck into the caravan and grab Alana and hold her to me.

"Are you okay?" I ask.

"Can I have cotton candy now?"

"You can have cotton candy and funnel cake and this sweet lady here can have anything she wants too."

5

Later that night, with Alana on the couch beside me watching YouTube videos, I pull out one of the old tattered folders and begin rereading articles and reports about Kaylee's case.

Seeing Scotty stirred everything back up and with the documentary shooting and the upcoming anniversary, I think it's time for Blade and I to finally do what we've been saying we're going to do and reinvestigate her case.

I start with a printout of an online article from a popular true crime web site.

Gone in the Night: The Disappearance of Kaylee Walsh

Nearly 10 years ago, near the tiny town of Dawson Falls, Georgia, a deep, dark, perplexing mystery began.

On April 9, 2014, 21-year-old Kaylee Walsh, a University of Florida psychology student, disappeared after a single car crash on Highway 69. Kaylee's disappearance has received worldwide exposure and is one of the most popular unsolved true crime cases in modern history.

In January 2014—three months before Kaylee's disappearance—she was arrested for a bar fight. In April she was arrested for public intoxication. In early March she and her boyfriend, Grant St. James, were involved in a car accident in his vehicle. It's suspected she was driving. In late March, Kaylee had an unreported, single car auto accident that left her vehicle damaged but drivable.

On April 7, 2014, Kaylee's dad, Benjamin, arrived in Gainesville, where Kaylee was a junior in college. He and Kaylee went car shopping that afternoon, and later, they went to dinner with a friend of his daughter.

Kaylee dropped her father off at his hotel room and borrowed his car to return to the campus for a dorm party. She arrived at the party at 10:30 p.m. She left the party on Sunday, April 8 at 2:30 a.m. At approximately 3:30 a.m., she was returning to her father's hotel and hit a guardrail on State Road 76 just outside of Gainesville, causing nearly $10,000 worth of damage to his new Cadillac CTS.

The responding officer wrote a report, but there is no mention of a sobriety test. Kaylee continued to her father's hotel and stayed in his room. Later, at 4:49 a.m., Kaylee made a phone call to her boyfriend from Benjamin's phone.

Later Sunday morning, Benjamin rented a vehicle, dropped off Kaylee back at the UF campus, and returned to Panama City. At about 11:30 p.m. that night, Benjamin called Kaylee and reminded her to get the accident forms so he could process his insurance claim for her accident. They agreed they would talk again on Monday.

I stop reading and look up, then pause the video on the screen.

"How are you sweet girl?" I ask.

"Good."

"You hungry or thirsty or anything?"

"No."

"Would you like to talk about what happened tonight?"

"Huh?"

"Were you scared?"

"Bruh," she says, sounding like a teenager, "I knew you and Blade had it."

"I'll always do everything I can to protect you."

She nods. "Can you turn the TV back on?"

"Sure."

She returns to her viewing and I return to my reading.

After midnight on Monday, April 9, Kaylee went on her computer and searched MapQuest for directions to Dahlonega and Helen, Georgia.

The first contact with Kaylee that day was at 1 p.m. when she emailed her boyfriend. She said:

"I got your messages, but honestly, I don't feel like talking. I really don't have anything to say. I'm sure we'll talk at some point. Until then, Kaylee."

Kaylee called a cabin rental agency in Dahlonega, Georgia, to inquire about renting a cabin. It was the same area where her family had previously vacationed. Records reflect the call lasted three minutes. Later, at 1:13 p.m., Kaylee called another student she went to college with.

At about 1:30 p.m., she emailed her professor that she needed to leave because there had been a death in the family. According to her family, no death had occurred.

She packed her bags into her 2010 Toyota Corolla sedan and went to the bank at 3:40 p.m. to withdraw most of the money from her account. With the $280 she withdrew, she purchased alcohol, including Bailey's Irish Cream, Kahlua, vodka, and a box of Franzia wine. Surveillance footage confirmed she was alone when she went to the bank and the liquor store.

She also picked up the accident report forms from the Motor Vehicle Registry sometime during the day.

Classes at the college were canceled due a bomb threat the day Kaylee disappeared. It is believed she left Gainesville around 1:45 p.m., likely via Interstate 75 north. She hadn't told anyone of her destination, nor was there any proof she had selected a place.

Approximately eight hours after she left Florida, the Dawson Falls Police Department received a 911 call from a resident reporting a car crash.

A woman who lived just outside of Dawson Falls, Georgia, heard a loud noise outside her house. She looked out the window and saw a car had missed the hairpin turn and had crashed into a stand of pines along Highway 69, also called Wildwood Road. The car was on the eastbound side of the road, pointed west.

The woman called the police Department at 8:28 p.m., reporting on the sharp corner neighboring her home. The woman also said she thought she saw a man inside the vehicle smoking a cigarette.

Another witness, a truck driver who lived nearby, stopped at the car. He could see the vehicle and a young woman walking around the car.

A silver 2010 Toyota Corolla that is identical to the car Kaylee was driving that fateful night.

The truck driver told police the young woman didn't have any injuries he could see, but she did appear to be upset and shaken up. He offered for her to come with him to his house, which was just across the way. When she declined, he offered to call for help, she told him she already had and that AAA was on the way. She pleaded with him not to call the police. Though he didn't say anything to her at the time, he later told police that he knew she was lying because there was no cell service in the area.

Another local driving home from work claims she passed by the scene around 8:37 p.m. and saw a police SUV parked head-to-head with Kaylee's car. She did not see anyone inside or outside the vehicles at the scene, so she continued home.

However, police records reflect the Dawson Falls Police Department arrived nine minutes later, contradicting the timeline the witness reported.

According to the official log, police arrived at 8:46 p.m. The officer on scene reported that no one was present, noting he believed the driver fled the scene to avoid a DUI. The car had hit a tree on the driver's side, knocking the radiator into the fan and damaging the left headlight, making the vehicle inoperable. There was a large, round crack in the windshield on the driver's side and both airbags had been deployed. Oddly the car was locked.

The officer saw red stains that looked like red wine spilled inside and outside the car. Inside on the back seat, he found an empty beer bottle and the box of wine Kaylee had purchased. He found her AAA card, blank accident report forms, CDs, a favorite stuffed animal, diamond jewelry, makeup, a printed map to Dahlonega, Georgia, and "Stolen: Innocence Lost," a book about sex trafficking. Kaylee's debit and credit cards were missing, along with her cellphone. Some of the bottles of liquor she purchased earlier that day also seemed to be missing.

Police initially classified Kaylee as a missing person and treated the case like she may have disappeared voluntarily. They could find no evidence of foul play.

A contractor who was going home from work between approximately 8 and 8:30 p.m. claimed he saw a young woman jogging east on Highway 69 about five miles away from where police found Kaylee's car. He said the person wore a dark coat with a lighter hoodie and jeans.

On April 10, police issued a BOLO alert for Kaylee and left a voicemail on Benjamin's home phone informing him that the car had been found deserted. Because he was working out of state, Benjamin never received that call.

At 5 p.m., Kaylee's brother called his father and informed him about Kaylee's accident and disappearance. He immediately contacted the Dawson Falls police and was told that the Georgia Department of Natural Resources would begin search efforts if Kaylee were not found by the following morning.

Kaylee's father and mother and siblings arrived in Dawson Falls before dawn on April 11. By 8:00 a.m., DNR investigators and the Walsh's were searching the woods for her. The K-9 unit on scene picked up a scent that led 100 yards away from the vehicle but then disappeared.

Later that afternoon, Kaylee's boyfriend, Grant St. James, arrived in Dawson Falls. St. James was in Miami at the time of Kaylee's disappearance. As soon as he returned, he drove up to meet the Walshes and to help with the search. He spent all afternoon and evening in the woods searching for Kaylee, and later that night when he was back at the hotel and had signal again, he checked his voicemail messages and discovered he had received a call from someone sobbing that he believed was Kaylee. Police traced the call to an American Red Cross calling card issued to people in crisis.

By April 12, Benjamin, Kay, Scotty and Kaylee's boyfriend conducted a press conference. Several national news agencies covered the story. Police announced that Kaylee may be on foot in the area and may be endangered and potentially suicidal.

The FBI joined the search 10 days after Kaylee's disappearance, and DNR then conducted another search by ground and air, using a helicopter equipped with a thermal imaging camera, search canines, and cadaver dogs.

At the end of April, police returned the items from Kaylee's car to her family.

When I close the folder and become aware of my surroundings again, Alana is asleep on the couch beside me, her little head resting on my leg, the TV is off, and the house is still and quiet.

"Come on, sweet girl, let's get you to bed."

In an instant an unwelcome thought invades my tired mind.

I imagine something happening to a twenty-one-year-old Alana similar to what happened to Kaylee.

Suddenly, I'm sweating and nauseated and can't catch my breath.

As I lift Alana up I hold her tightly to me, overwhelmed by a desire to protect her and keep her from harm.

It hits me so hard I'm trembling and finding it difficult to walk.

I feel for Benjamin and Kay to a depth and degree I never have before and realize I haven't empathized with them nearly enough. Until Alana I couldn't begin to understand or imagine the level of their loss and suffering.

I ease Alana down onto her bed, pulling the covers up around her and tucking her in.

Stepping into my room, I grab a pillow and blanket off my bed, and returning to Alana's room, not for the first time, sleep on the floor next to her bed.

6

On Monday morning, I meet with my therapist, Judah Kesler.

His office is in a small, converted, postwar wooden home in downtown on Grace Avenue.

He's a late-forties former surfer from Hawaii with long dark hair just starting to go gray. He's gentle and generous and soft-spoken.

I'm court ordered to see him, but I'd see him anyway.

He's intelligent and insightful and compassionate, and I find myself looking forward to our sessions all week.

"How was your weekend?" he asks.

"Eventful," I say and tell him.

"A very full and eventful weekend," he says.

His smallish office is a bit cluttered and smells faintly of scented candles and incense. A couple of bookshelves with too many books on them appear about ready to collapse. An old wooden desk on the back wall is marred and wobbly. I'm seated on a quilt-covered loveseat and he's across from me in a faded, worn, and misshapen recliner.

"I was . . . I felt good about not reacting in anger when I felt attacked by Blade," I say. "I had just enough space around it so I could pause a moment before responding. It was almost like I was observing myself or my thoughts and not just reacting."

"That's great. Why do you think that was?"

"Probably had a lot to do with it being Blade," I say.

"How so?"

"I'm . . . We're . . . I feel the closet to and safest with her. I know how she is. I wasn't surprised she felt that way. But I also think it was the practices I've been doing—especially the mindfulness meditation."

He nods and smiles. "That's . . . so good. Yes. And it's so good you recognize it and appreciate your growth. You've mentioned not reacting to the way she said what she said, but what did you think about what she actually said—the content?"

"I've never thought of myself as too nice."

"Why do you think she said it?"

"Compared to her I'm the nicest guy in the world," I say. "And she really thinks it. And . . . there may be something to it."

"What do you mean?"

"When she said it . . . it made me think. Maybe I am too nice sometimes."

"We all play different roles at different times," he says. "You and Blade form a family and have a dynamic. You have a role and she has a role—most likely ones you learned to play a very long time ago."

"That's true. I'm often more of a peacemaker when I'm around her than others."

"Do you feel like it's your responsibility to make peace? What would happen if you didn't?"

"We'd have less clients. We'd get less information. Solve less cases."

"So in the context of work it has a utilitarian purpose," he says.

I nod. "Definitely.

"Was the situation she was upset about work related?" he asks.

I stop and think about it, then shake my head. "No it wasn't. So . . . I must do it in general also, not just in the context of work."

"Do you know why you do it?"

"I didn't realize I did."

"Can you think about it and see if you can figure out why you might?"

I do.

"I guess—I don't guess, I know. I want to be liked, thought of as a good guy, not rejected."

"So the belief is . . . if I'm nice, helpful, a peacemaker, a good person . . . I won't be rejected. Is that it?"

I nod. "Somewhat, yeah. I mean, it's not just that. Some of it is just my nature and personality and . . . who I am. But, yeah."

"Given your early experiences it's not surprising you'd feel like you need to . . . could we call it . . . guard against rejection?"

I nod.

A piercing pain of abandonment stabs through my lower abdomen, a small child crying for a mommy who never comes, a vulnerable little boy without the protection and guidance of a dad.

"Why do you think that is?" he asks.

"You already said it," I say. "Early . . . I've never said it out loud . . . or even thought about it quite like this, but . . . being abandoned by your parents is the ultimate rejection."

"It makes sense that little Luc would want to do whatever he had to to make sure that never happened again."

I tried so hard not to be a bother for any family who was willing to take me in. I wouldn't ask for anything. I would thank them for anything they gave me or did for me. I'd try to always be pleasant and happy and mannerly and helpful. God, my heart breaks for that little boy.

I'm seeing things I've never seen before.

He waits, letting me sit with that insight for as long as I need to.

"I tried so hard to be liked and accepted in the foster homes I was put into," I say. "But no matter what I did . . . it didn't work."

"So you had the experience of being rejected over and over again?"

I nod slowly. "I did."

I think about Blade and how different we are. "I try to be liked so as not to be rejected and Blade . . . rejects others before they can reject her."

He nods. "Would you say it's two different approaches to a similar experience?"

I nod again and drop into silent reflection.

Eventually, I say, "How do I . . . What do I do about it?"

"What do you mean?"

"How do I stop being . . . too nice or a peacemaker or a people pleaser or whatever?"

"Do you want to?"

"It's unhealthy, isn't it?"

"Is it?" he asks. "It can be, of course. But nearly anything can be. There's nothing wrong with being nice or a peacemaker or caring a certain amount what others think. Probably only sociopaths don't. It's when we care too much what others think, when we feel a compulsion to be nice or liked. Now that you are aware of it . . . I'd say try to start noticing what is genuine and authentic and what is not. The more you heal, the more you love and accept yourself, the more inward-oriented you are, the less you will need or want or even care about the approval or acceptance of others. Then you can just be true to who you are, your nature, your personality. Notice if you start slipping into a role. Notice your motives—are you being kind because you are kind and that's who you are or are you trying to get something from someone—even if it's just their approval."

I smile and laugh a little.

"What is it?" he asks.

"I was just thinking how much I want your approval and realized just how far I have to go."

7

When I pull up to our office, I find Scotty waiting for me.

By the time I park and get out of my car he's standing there.

"Hey, Luc," he says. "How are you this morning?"

I nod. "Pretty good. You?"

"I'm . . . I feel bad about what happened this weekend and —well, and . . . really the past ten years. I'd like to . . . Do you and Blade have a few minutes?"

"Sure," I say, "come on in."

As he follows me into our building and back to our office I wonder if I'm being too nice and accommodating.

In the plush, impressive lobby, he whistles and says, "This is nice, man. Y'all are doing even better than I realized."

I shake my head. "It's the girlfriend experience."

"Huh? How so?"

"It's not real. We're only in this building because one of our foster brothers who's a non-partnered attorney here got us the hook up and we do some investigative work for them from time to time."

"Got me thinkin' I might need to reconsider the girlfriend experience."

In our office we find Blade behind the desk on her laptop.

She has earbuds in and is bobbing her head to a beat we can't hear.

As we each take a seat in the two client chairs across the desk from her she looks up, smiles, and shakes her head.

"Let me guess," she says to me, removing her earbuds, dropping them on the desk, and closing her computer, "you want us to adopt him."

"I found him loitering in the parking lot and made a citizens' arrest," I say.

Blade glances over at Scotty. "Look," she says, "I was too hard on you this weekend and I'm sorry, but that don't mean I want to make nice and start hangin' out and shit."

"I've just got a couple of things to say if you'll let me then I'll be gone."

"Okay," she says. "Let's hear it."

"First, I wanted to say how sorry I am. I know I was young, but . . . that's not an excuse. I only viewed Kaylee's disappearance for how it affected me. I . . . I didn't consider y'all enough. My folks didn't either. The truth is it fucked us all up. Not saying that as an excuse. It's just the facts. And if I'm keepin' completely real . . . they haven't had much to give me since it happened."

"Oh, you poor thing," Blade says.

"That's not what I'm saying. Just wanted y'all to know it wasn't personal. They are shadows of themselves. Shells. Anyway . . . I'm sorry. And they are too."

Blade nods. "It fucked us all up. Facts."

He's not going to get much more than that and seems to know it.

"The other thing is . . ." he says. "I know you said you wouldn't let us hire you to find out what happened to Kaylee, but . . . I was thinkin' . . . it's going to take a lot of resources, right? So at first . . . I thought . . . I was going to see if I could partner with you and pay for DNA testing or whatever else was needed. That kind of thing, but then I thought about the documentary they're doing and I had an idea."

He pauses and looks from Blade to me.

I nod encouragingly.

"I know they asked y'all to be on it," he says. "They asked us too. I think we probably gave them the same response. But I was thinkin . . . what if they foot the bill for your investigation?"

"Why would they do that?" Blade asks.

"Because you wouldn't just be interviewed for it, you'd be the stars. The show would be your investigation."

Blade shakes her head. "They won't go for that."

"Actually . . . they already did," he says. "I spoke to the producer this morning. It's yours if you want it."

"Bullshit," Blade says.

"Truth," he says.

"Why would they—How'd you get them to go for that?"

"Told them it was the only way to get the family to be involved," he says. "They get us all or they get none of us."

It's his way of saying we're family again.

Blade looks away. I blink several times.

"They get access to the family if it's her family that's conducting the investigation. Y'all call the shots. No interference. They get to follow you, film you, but that's it. And for that they'll not only finance the investigation but pay you a shit ton to do it. We're talkin' TV money. That's the biggest best money there is."

"Scotty," I say.

He looks over at me.

"Scott, I mean. Thank you. That was a hell of a thing for you to do."

Blade nods. "Whether we do it or not, we appreciate what you've done."

"Of course," he says. "Wish I had done a lot more a long time ago, but . . . I hope y'all will do it. I really do. I think it would be best for Kaylee, for y'all, for all of us. The producers are ready to meet. We have to move fast because with or without us they're airing it on her anniversary."

8

"How much you think TV money really is?" Blade says.

"A lot."

"That's what I've heard."

I say, "Means a lot that he did it."

"Whatcha think?" she says. "Should we do it?"

"We're gonna do it," I say. "Question is . . . we gonna do it with them or on our own."

"That's only true if we're doin' it now," she says. "If we doin' it later . . . then the question answers itself."

I nod. "Only one reason to wait, right?"

"One big one."

If we wait until I'm off probation the investigation will be a hell of a lot easier to conduct and I'd be legally permitted to travel to the places we need to go—namely Gainesville and Dawson Falls.

I say, "Wonder how much they'll interfere?"

"*Try* to interfere," she says.

"Thing is . . . even if they don't try to direct the investigation . . . they can cut the documentary any way they want to. They can make us look any way they want to. They can make anyone look guilty or not."

"But . . . that's got nothin' to do with our investigation."

"Depending on what they do . . . it could be used by a defense attorney to get the guilty guy off."

She nods but doesn't say anything and I know what she's thinking.

She doesn't think it'll ever make it to trial.

"Won't matter who they say did it," she says, "as long as who actually did it is deep in the ground of a north Georgia pine forest."

"So we doin' it?" I ask.

"You the one riskin' prison. Think you should decide."

"Let's at least meet with the producer and see what kind of read we get."

9

"True crime is the quickest growing genre in the 21st century," Karen McKeithen is saying. "People love it. We are fascinated by it —not as much for the gory details, although some readers and viewers love that too—but for the inside look into abnormal psychology. Our industry is booming."

Karen McKiethen is a middle-aged blond-haired white woman with pale skin and lots of makeup in a navy-blue pantsuit.

In her youth, she was a documentary filmmaker of some acclaim. These days she's doing more producing than directing and her speciality is the enormously popular true crime genre.

Blade and I are in our office meeting with her via Zoom on Blade's laptop. The door is closed and we are seated next to each other behind our desk.

We do very little work here at the office. Most of our work is done in the field. Our office is primarily for meetings. It looks like a set more than an actual workplace—especially since the furnishing and decorations came with it.

"Do you know that half of Americans say they enjoy true

crime and 13% say it's their favorite? And of course women can't get enough of it—58% of women say it's their favorite while only 42% of men."

"That's 'cause so many men too busy practicing it," Blade says.

"Too true," Karen says. "Too too true. One in three Americans say they consume true-crime content at least once per week, while 24% say they do multiple times per week. Of course, I'm sure I don't have to tell you all this. You are on the front lines living it every day, aren't you?"

"Too true," Blade says. "Too too true."

Karen pauses a moment and seems to be trying to determine if she's being mocked.

"As I mentioned to you when we spoke before . . ." she says. "I have a production deal with Investigation Discovery. I'm producing a documentary on Kaylee that is scheduled to air on the tenth anniversary of her disappearance."

"Sorry about before," I say. "We were involved in a series of ongoing cases that had us scrambling, so we weren't sure we'd have time to be involved."

"And now?"

In her best white girl finishing school voice Blade says, "Our schedule is . . . more amenable."

"Obviously, the documentary is already in production, but we can pivot to you two and your investigation, but we'd have to move fast. Is that possible? Are you in a position to do a full-scale investigation into this case? How long would it take you to get up to speed?"

"Oh, we up to speed," Blade says.

I say, "We've been living with and working this case for nearly a decade."

"That's right. You have a connection to the victim."

"Her family took us in," I say. "They were our foster family for a few years."

"Oh, my God, that's perfect. What an angle."

Blade says, "Just so we clear . . . We're talkin' about an actual investigation, not some staged TV bullshit, right?"

"Oh, absolutely. We want you all to solve the case. You would do what you normally do in a case like this. We would observe and film and then interview you afterwards."

"And if a situation is too dangerous?" I say. "Or the presence of cameras would hinder the investigation?"

"Then we hang back and either shoot some footage when you're done or just interview you about it with some B-roll footage."

"And," Blade says, "we'd have a contract that spells all this out?"

"Absolutely."

I say, "Would we have any say in what is included in the documentary?"

"Of course. Not final cut or anything, but we'd welcome your input."

Blade says, "And this is all to secure the involvement of the family?"

She shakes her head. "No. That is a part of it, but . . . Remember . . . I came to you months ago. I'm aware of your work. The family connection is undeniably brilliant and will make for a compelling hook, but . . . Let me tell you two something. You have exactly what we're looking for. You're young and attractive and diverse and experienced. You're good at what you do and are going to work well for this format. Women are going to love you, Mr. Burke. And . . . Ms. Blade . . . you are a very colorful and compelling character. What you both bring is . . . what I'm looking for. And what I would want from you is to be yourselves and do your work as usual. Forget about the cameras and the production and solve this case. Can you do that?"

"You bet your skinny white ass we can," Blade says.

"Well, that's what I'm doing, so good. And let me say this. I've told you what you can do for the show. Now let me tell you what I can do for you. It is not hyperbole to say that this is the greatest opportunity of your careers. You will be paid more than you ever have been on any case. I guarantee it. And you'll have a budget for your investigation and resources like you've only dreamed of. And . . . if this goes the way I believe it will . . . you could have a career in this. We're talkin' the big boys. Your next production could be with Netflix or HBO."

"We have careers," Blade says. "Ain't lookin' to be movie stars. Truth is . . . that would hinder our work. All we lookin' to do is use your resources to aid our investigation. All we want to do is find our sister."

"Well, I'm your best chance of doing that. Do we have a deal?"

When we end the call a few moments later, I say, "Whatta you think?"

Blade says, "Can't be as good as she's sayin', but . . . if it's anywhere close . . . be our best bet to find her."

I nod.

She says, "And if TV money is good as they say . . ."

"Then we can provide for Alana's future," I say.

"Yeah, that's what I was gonna say."

"So we doin' it?"

She nods. "If your new probation officer will let you."

10

My new probation officer is a mild-mannered middle-aged man. He seems honest and genuinely decent. He's a by-the-book bureaucrat, but I could've done a lot worse.

His office is what you'd expect, about as vanilla as you can get—and with nothing personal in it. No family photos, of course, but also no framed diplomas or awards or citations.

I sit across his desk from him while he peruses my file.

This is my first time meeting with him, and it makes me miss Lexi and wonder what might have been.

Because of my anger issues, my series of assaults and many simple batteries, and my history of violence, when I committed aggravated battery on a suspect, a truly evil sociopath named Logan Owens, I was charged with a felony and sent to prison. Because my sentencing score sheet was so high, the judge sentenced me to a year and a day of state prison time, followed by two years of probation. If I ever violate my probation, I'll return to prison to serve my full sentence as well as any additional time I might pick up from the act that violated me back in the first place.

"Your previous probation officer had glowing things to say about you in her reports," he says. You're in counseling and an anger management support group?"

I nod. "Yes, sir."

"How are they going?"

"I'm getting a lot more out of the therapy than the support group, but they both help."

"And your job and living situation?"

I tell him.

He nods as I speak and takes notes. "Sounds like you have a good family support system and work situation."

"I do."

"My only concern would be the type of work you do bringing you into situations of violence."

"I'm very careful," I lie. "Mostly what I do is in the office instead of the field."

"That's good. I'll drop in soon and visit you at work and your home."

I nod.

"Any questions for me?" he asks. "Any way I can help you succeed?"

"I wanted to talk to you about a couple of travel permits," I say.

"Okay," he says. "If it's for leisure or pleasure and you're behind on restitution payments . . . the answer will have to be no."

"It's for work," I say.

"And you're not on house arrest and don't have a curfew?"

"Right."

"In state or out of state?" he asks.

"One of each," I say. "Gainesville, Florida first and then Dawson Falls, Georgia."

"In state is less involved, but for both I need to know where you'll be staying and be able to verify it. Will you be accompanied by someone?"

"Yes, sir. My partner in the agency and foster sister, Alix Baker."

"I'll have to verify everything with her also. You'll still have to check in like usual. I can give you verbal approval for Gainesville, but for Georgia you're going to have to fill out a form, which includes a waiver of extradition agreement and it will have to be approved not just by me but the probation supervisor as well. If you'll be in either place more than 48 hours you'll have to register with the sheriff's office."

"What's the nature of the work?"

I tell him about Kaylee and our connection to her and our intention to find out what happened to her.

He nods slowly. "That's good. I hope y'all do. I really do."

11

Kaylee's case has two main mysteries and many, many smaller ones.

Obviously, what happened to her is the most pressing and important one, but why she was even up there in the first place is also perplexing.

Then, of course, there's the baffling mystery of how she could've vanished so quickly while eyewitnesses were watching.

Why did she do what she did? Why leave without telling anyone and why go where she was going?

The accepted timeline is as follows:

Friday, April 6th, 2014

10:10 p.m. – Kaylee talks to her cousin Kaitlin, who is like a sister to her.

12:07 a.m. – Kaylee calls her boyfriend, Grant.

12:20 a.m. – Officers discover Blake Christie, a UF student, lying in the road after a hit and run.

1:00 a.m. – Dorm Supervisor, Jennifer Jackson, arrives and witnesses Kaylee's strange behavior. She is upset and nearly catatonic. Her only utterance is "Kaitlin."

1:15 a.m. Jennifer escorts Kaylee to her dorm room.

Saturday, April 7th, 2014

Ben Walsh arrives at UF to go car shopping with Kaylee. Ben later tells police in an interview that on his way to UF that weekend he stopped at several ATMs to withdraw $400, totaling 4k.

3:31 p.m. – Kaylee calls her brother Scotty.

6:00 p.m. – Kaylee, Ben, and Kaylee's friend, Brandi Martin, have dinner together at the Oak, a restaurant in downtown Gainesville.

After Dinner, Kaylee, Ben, and Brandi go to a liquor store to purchase alcohol. The two girls then drop Ben off at his hotel and use his car to attend a party at the dorms.

Sunday, April 8th, 2014

3:30 a.m. – Kaylee is in an accident in her father's vehicle.

4:49 a.m. – Kaylee arrives at her Dad's hotel room.

5:00 a.m. – Kaylee calls Grant.

10:00 a.m. Ben departs Gainesville to return to Panama City.

Monday, April 9th, 2014

12:00 a.m. – Kaylee searches places to stay in Helen and Dahlonega, Georgia.

10:00 a.m. – Kaylee emails Grant she doesn't feel like talking right now, but will call him later.

11:30 a.m. – Kaylee emails her professors and work supervisor to say she will be gone for a few days because of a death in the family.

1:00 p.m. – Kaylee leaves campus in her car, which is in need of repair.

1:15 p.m. – Kaylee stops at an ATM near campus and withdraws $680.00

1:43 p.m. – Kaylee stops by a liquor store and purchases a large quantity of alcohol.

2:30 p.m. – Kaylee attempts to call her mother, Kay, but gets no response.

4:37 p.m. – Kaylee calls her dorm voicemail to check her messages.

7:27 p.m. – Hope Westmacott calls 911 after hearing Kaylee's crash and looking out her window.

7:30 p.m. – Bruce Lewis a truck driver who lives across from where Kaylee crashed stops to check on her.

7:43 p.m. – Lewis calls 911 from his home.

7:46 p.m. – The first officer responds to the scene. Kaylee is not there. Her car is locked.

7:54 p.m. – BOLO Issued (5'7, female, on foot, victim of crash)

9:50 p.m. – The final first responder clears the scene.

Tuesday, April 10th, 2014

Ben receives a call from a Dawson Falls police detective about the wreck and abandoned vehicle. He tells the investigator that Kaylee has been down and depressed and not in a good way and he was concerned she might be trying to hurt herself.

12

Bloom is a women's boutique in a restored old building on Harrison Avenue in Downtown Panama City not far from the old Sherman Arcade building. It's sandwiched between a salon and a skateboard shop.

The bloom motif is everywhere—in the form of open and opening flowers. They're plastered on the walls, the canvas shopping bags, the gift cards, even the receipt paper. Large fake flowers in old metal pails, buckets, and vases are also scattered throughout the shop, mostly on top of the round industrial clothing racks.

The boutique is owned by Brandi Martin, one of Kaylee's closest friends—and the only one from high school who was also at UF with her.

She's an early thirties new mom in stylish clothes that nearly conceal she hasn't lost her pregnancy weight yet.

Seeing her I can't help but think that Kaylee would be this age now, which is hard to imagine and reminds me that she's perpetually a twenty-one-year-old in my mind. Like Brandi, she would likely have had children by now. She's missed so much. *We've* missed so much.

Bloom isn't open yet. Blade, Brandi, and I are the only ones in the shop. When we arrived Brandi had been pulling random winter dresses from various places around the store and moving them to the sale rack in the back. There are only a few of each style of winter dress left, and they appear to be either very small or very large.

She says, "We have to buy each garment in a package that goes from extra small to like XXL or bigger. The mediums, larges, and smalls, which there are more of, usually sell very well, but the ones on the extreme ends—the real small or real large—almost never do."

The three of us are now standing around the sale rack.

"I like your style," she says, raising her eyebrows and nodding appreciatively to Blade. "Wish I could carry clothes like those in here. Can you imagine?" She shakes her head and smiles mischievously. "Anyway . . . Can y'all tell I'm stalling? I still have such a hard time talking about what happened to Kaylee. Still feel so raw."

Her eyes glisten and she sniffles, but no tears fall.

"I've thought about it so much over the years," she is saying. "Trying to see what I missed. I still can't believe it really happened. It's like a bad dream that I remember less and less of each year. Like it happened to someone else. It's hard to explain."

I nod.

"After all this time . . . all the time I've spent thinking about it . . . I have nothing new to add. Haven't come up with anything."

I say, "Don't feel pressured to come up with something new."

"Only pressure I feel is what I put on myself. I just feel so bad, like I wasn't a good friend . . . like I was too self-involved to really see what was going on with her."

"So you think something *was* going on with her before she went missing?" I ask.

She nods. "Yeah. Didn't seem like a big deal . . . until she . . . until she went missing."

"How long before she went missing would you say whatever it was was going on?"

She shrugs. "A few months maybe."

"Tell us what she was like before then. Before she changed."

"She was a lot like she was in high school. She didn't change much. Lots of the girls went a little crazy. Away from home for the first time. Suddenly, all this freedom. Drinking. Partying. Hoookin' up. Not Kaylee. Don't get me wrong. She was social and had a good time, but she didn't lose her way, herself. She was one of the genuinely sweetest people I've ever met. Truly kind. Even the good girls, the nice girls—and I include myself in that group—were still so self-centered and immature. Sort of silly. Kaylee was never like that. She was levelheaded too. Just sort of calm and steady and caring. When we first got down there . . . I went a little wild. Nothing too crazy, but I was drinking way too much. Hookin' up . . . more than I care to remember. I started missing classes, not finishing assignments. Kaylee and I stopped hanging for a while. Not her. She didn't stop hanging with me. I stopped hanging with her. We were just headed in such different directions. And I felt guilty. I thought she was a goody-goody and . . . But she never stopped being kind to me. And when I got through that initial wild child stage she was just the same and we became close again. She was such a good, stable person. Came from a good family—I mean, y'all know that. We used to say she wasn't crazy enough to become a psychologist."

Blade nods and says, "Lots of family members and friends of missing or murdered people remember whitewashed versions of the person that sanitize and sanctify them. She lit up every room she walked into. He was always so kind. But we know what you sayin' about Kaylee is absolutely true."

"And yet," I say, "at a certain point something changed."

Brandi nods. "I'm not saying she changed or that any of the things I've said about her weren't true anymore. But you could tell she was going through something. She was a little more withdrawn. She had a . . . I'd say she was a little less joyful. It's hard to explain, but it was like . . . the closest thing I can think of is . . . it was like she had a headache."

I nod and think about it. No one's ever described it like that before—not even Brandi.

"She started getting into a little trouble," she continues. "Nothing major, but still . . . it was a change. And . . . but . . . it was weird. It wasn't like she had changed. It was like she was the same, sweet Kaylee but with a headache and getting into trouble."

"What did you think it was at the time?" I ask. "What do you think it was now?"

She shrugs. "I thought . . . I guess back then I thought it was Grant. Her boyfriend. He was . . . He wasn't on the same level as her. He was . . . He was fucked up and it was like she was trying to help him. I guess I thought he was getting into trouble and she was just there—you know, like an innocent bystander. But why was she even with him? How could she stay? Maybe she just couldn't figure out a way to get out of the relationship or . . . maybe she thought she would save him. I don't know. I guess I thought she was drinkin' too much too. She was never a big drinker. I never saw her drunk. She'd have a drink or two if we went out, but never had too much. But when she started getting into fights and wrecks . . . I thought maybe she was drinking or on something. A lot of students were takin' speed and Ritalin and other things to help them stay up to study and to party and still get to class. She was a good student. I thought maybe she was putting too much pressure on herself. Or that Grant was getting her drunk or high to more easily control her. But . . . I was around her a lot. Nearly everyday. Usually several hours everyday. At different times during the day—morning, afternoon, evening, late night. I never ever . . . not once saw her intoxicated. Never once thought she was on something. So . . . the truth is . . . I don't know what to think. Ten years . . . and I haven't come to any new conclusions."

"And you had no idea she was leaving?" I ask.

She shakes her head. "None. I was shocked—as much about not even knowing she was gone as what happened to her. I was right across the hall. I thought it was odd that I didn't see her that night. Figured she and Grant were together and I'd see her the next morning. I texted her a few times and usually no matter what was going on she'd text me back at some point, but that night it was just . . . crickets. Even as I was going to bed I figured when I woke up I'd have a text from her waiting on me. Instead I got a call from her dad asking if I had heard from her or knew anything about where she was. It was like I woke up in a nightmare and have never quite been able to get out of it."

"I'm sure you've heard all the rumors and theories swirling around out there?"

"I don't follow the case," she says. "Haven't listened to any of the podcasts or anything, but I've still heard way too much over the years."

"One of them was that she was running from Grant," I say. "Do you think she could've been?"

She shrugs. "I guess it's possible, but I didn't see anything that makes me think that's what she was doing. He was a mess. What college kid isn't? Insecure and controlling. But from what I could see she had the power in the relationship. That's why he was insecure. To me . . . from what I could see he was sort of sad and pathetic. There was no abuse. Nothing physical or anything. And they seemed really crazy about each other. If they broke up . . . it'd be her breaking up with him and if she did his response would've been to beg her back, but not to hurt her. I could be wrong, but . . . that's how I saw it then and that hasn't changed."

"What about the rumor that she was having an affair with one of her professors?"

She nods. "I've heard that one too. Andrew Collins. I don't know. She never said anything to me and I never saw anything that would make me think they were, but . . . they were close. He was her advisor and mentor, but I think that was it. If it was more . . . she did a fantastic job of hiding it."

"Have you stayed in touch with the family?"

She gives a slight tilt of her head and a half-frown. "Sort of. Not really. They are . . . so broken and . . . her parents, I mean. Scotty's okay. But they . . . it's like they disappeared with her. I've tried to reach out, keep in touch, but never got a lot of response and haven't tried in a while. Is it the same for y'all?"

I nod, not wanting to get into our lack of relationship with these people who used to be our family.

"I'm glad Scotty is havin' some semblance of a life. Kaylee would want that. No matter what happened to her. She'd want that for her parents too, but I get why they can't."

"How 'bout Blake Christie?" Blade says.

"Who?"

"Dude who got run over."

A few days before Kaylee disappeared, a UF student was the victim of a hit-and-run. Shortly after it happened was when Kaylee was found nearly catatonic by her supervisor, Jennifer Jackson.

I add, "Some speculate she hit him, which was why she was so upset and why she ran away."

"Oh, yeah, well . . . I don't know. On the one hand she was supposed to be at work. But I know she would slip out sometimes. They all did."

Kaylee's job was to sit at the desk in the entry way to her

dorm during the night shift. She was there to buzz residents in and out and check their IDs, to call campus security when necessary, to provide information and assistance when needed. It was an easy job that allowed her to study and complete homework assignments while being paid.

"On the one hand," Brandi continues, "her driving was so erratic during that time—accident after accident—but on the other . . . she was not the type of person who would flee a scene. She just wasn't. She was one of the most caring and compassionate people I ever met. The timing is suspicious . . . and I see why it's a popular theory for true crimers, but . . . I don't know. There's no evidence is there? What did the victim say?"

"He was in a coma for a good while," I say. "When he finally woke up . . . he couldn't remember anything. And no, I don't think there's any direct evidence."

"And didn't she . . ." she says. "The night that it happened. When Jennifer found her so upset, didn't she say *Kaitlin*?"

I nod. "She did. Any idea why?"

"Kaylee was one of the kindest people I've ever met. Truly, authentically, sweet. She collected strays—or they were drawn to her . . . Kaitlin was her cousin. They grew up together and were close, but . . . Kaitlin was a mess. Always in crises. Kaylee was like her sponsor, her counselor, her . . . really about her only friend. I'm sure something Kaitlin was going through upset her, but I have no idea what it was."

13

City Arts Cooperative is tucked away in an old building on a side street in downtown Panama City. Located on Luverne next to the boxing club and across from McKenzie Park, City Arts is a space where member artists can create, collaborate, perform, display, and teach. Equipped with gallery space, classrooms, and a dance floor, there's always something creative happening at City Arts.

Kaylee's cousin, Kaitlin Walsh, is a member. We find her here working on a painting before she goes to her server job at the House of Henry, the Irish Pub and Sports Bar on Harrison. She's been a server all of her adult life. It's all she's ever done. You'd think she'd be good at it by now, but she's far too self-involved and unstable. She never lasts any place long and soon she'll have worked her way through every eating establishment in Panama City.

She's sitting on the floor, her legs wide apart and a canvas between them. She's working on what might be an impressionistic painting of St. Andrew Bay.

I say might be because it's so impressionistic it could be nearly anything—except art.

I vaguely remember learning something about virtuoso brushwork in my high school art class or a book I read in prison. For many great artists the brush is like an extension of their arm.

That's definitely not the case for Kaitlin.

There's no flow to her work, and she seems to paint thick when it should be smooth and vice versa. She appears incapable of being delicate or blending different techniques and her use of color makes me wonder if she might actually be colorblind.

As far as I can tell we're alone in the building.

"We were like sisters," she is saying while continuing to paint. "Closer than sisters. Closer than anybody. What happened to her . . . is the worst thing that ever happened to me."

"Pretty bad for her too," Blade says.

Kaitlin stops painting and looks up at her. "Well, yeah, of course . . . Unless . . ."

We have remained standing and are towering over her.

"Unless?" I ask.

"Unless she just walked out of her life and started over," she says returning her attention to her canvas.

"You think she did?" Blade asks.

"I would," she says. "I really would. Get away from all the pressure put on her. Get away from the men in her life who were constantly tryin' to control her. Go away and have her baby in peace."

"Her *baby*?" Blade says.

"She was pregnant?" I ask.

"I think so."

"What makes you think that?" I ask.

"Just a feeling—from knowing her so well."

"Did she say or do anything to make you think she might be?" I ask.

"No. It's just my intuition."

Kaitlin Walsh is a mess. Her unkempt hair spills out of her bandana do rag, and her wrinkled, baggie jean jumpsuit is painted-spattered and soiled. She appears to be attempting to strike the pose of an artist, but her painting suggests she has no actual artistic ability.

"You said you *would* think she walked out of her life," I say. "Does that mean you don't think she did?"

"I think she was tryin' to, but something happened. Somebody got to her. Because she would never start over without letting me know. I think she was going to contact me to join her once she got settled, but . . . never got the chance."

Blade starts to say something but Kaitlin cuts her off.

"Wait, are you the two foster kids they took in for a while? You are, aren't you? I knew you seemed . . . You've grown up, but I can still see some of the kids you used to be. Y'all turned out good, didn't you? Actual private investigators and all? Wow. They really saved y'all, didn't they?"

"Yeah," Blade says. "We owe everything to them."

Too obtuse to pick up on the sarcasm, Kaitlin says, "No wonder you're tryin' to help them find out what happened to Kaylee. I hope you can. I really do. But . . . I'm afraid she'll never be found."

From somewhere upstairs someone begins playing a trumpet. Evidently, we're not alone in the building.

"You spoke to her a few days before she disappeared," I say.

"We used to talk all the time. We were like sisters."

"It was a little after ten on that Friday night," I say. "Do you remember the conversation?"

She shakes her head. "We talked all the time—about everything. No telling. Probably just what was going on in our lives at the time. We shared everything."

"She was very upset that night," I say. "Did she mention why?"

She shakes her head. "If she did . . . I don't recall. Probably something stupid Grant did."

"A little while later she was so upset she could hardly speak. When her supervisor asked her what was wrong she just whispered your name."

"She probably wanted to talk to me again, wanted me to help her calm down or something."

"Did she mention Blake Christie?"

She shakes her head again. "No. Who is he? A guy she was interested in?"

"UF student who was hit by a car that night."

"Oh. No. She didn't say anything about him. Least not that I remember."

"Did you tell her something upsetting that night?" I ask. "Did you have anything going on that would make her upset or worried about you?"

"Probably," she says. "I've had a shit life. Didn't get any of the . . . advantages she and Scotty did. But I don't remember what it would've been. Take your pick—abusive boyfriend, screwed over by a friend, losin' a job, not havin' my art gettin' the recognition it deserves."

Blade starts to say something, which I know will be funny and truthful, but won't help the interview, so I say, "Do you remember what was going on with Kaylee in general during the time right before she vanished?"

She shrugs. "We mostly talked about me."

"Shocker," Blade says.

Ignoring her, Kaitlin continues, "She had a pretty stable, boring life. It was mine that was interesting and . . . exciting. I'm sure she was dealin' with Grant bein' a jerk. He was . . . She brought him home one time and we went out. The creep hit on me. My cousin who's like a sister to me is in the next room and he's tryin' to get with me. Wasn't surprising, but still . . . Seems like she wasn't feeling too good. She wrecked her car, I think.

Grant got into a fight with this dude and his girlfriend jumped Kaylee. I think. One of her . . . something about one of her professors . . . trying to fuck her . . . maybe. I don't know. I can't remember what was when."

"Do you remember the professor's name?"

She shakes her head. "Not a chance."

"Not a surprise," Blade says.

She stops painting and looks up at us. "Y'all ever wonder why they took you in?"

"No," Blade says, "it never crossed our minds."

"What if it was to make up for something? You know . . . do a good deed because of some bad ones. What if they're not the perfect little family?"

"Do you know something?" I ask. "Or are you just—"

"Just asking the question," she says. "Something was up with Kaylee. What if her dad . . ."

"There's absolutely no indication that anything like that is true," I say.

"I know, but I'm just saying. What was she doing up there? Why didn't she tell anyone? Why was she fuckin' up her life? What was with all the wrecks? It was probably Grant. But if it wasn't . . . Or why was she with someone like him in the first place? And what about the professor? Had to be daddy issues, right?"

Blade says, "Ever heard of projection?"

"Huh?"

I say, "She's saying you're a better painter than psychologist."

"And," Blade adds, "you're a fuckin' horrible painter."

14

Benjamin Walsh is a tall, thin, mid-fifties man with thinning, graying hair and a closely trimmed gray beard. His kind blue eyes are reservoirs of pain and wisdom. He's gentle and soft-spoken, measured and deliberate. He's nearly never in a hurry.

He's a highly respected family law attorney known for compassion, fairness, and integrity.

We are in his home office on Beach Drive, the front of which is tinted glass with a stunning view of the bay.

He's in a large, plush, leather, high-back chair behind his enormous dark wood desk, the wall behind him filled with barrister bookcases lined with Florida law books. The wall to his left is filled with degrees and awards and citations. The one to his right holds family photos, including the last one they ever took a few weeks before Kaylee vanished. Though at one time there were, there are no longer any photos of me and Blade in the room.

I say, "We were hoping to speak with you and Kay."

He nods. "I know. And I'm sorry. But she's not able to just yet."

I nod my understanding. Blade shakes her head and lets out a little sigh.

She's showing more deference and less overt hostility toward Ben than she did Scotty, but her anger still simmers just beneath the surface.

She says, "She still not able to talk about it after ten years?"

Ignoring her question, Ben says, "Before we begin . . . I want to say again how sorry I am for what happened. We made many mistakes after we lost Kaylee, but perhaps the biggest—certainly the one I regret the most—was how we . . . failed you two. I can't begin to tell you how terrible I feel. And before anything else . . . I want to ask for your forgiveness."

"Again?" Blade says.

He looks at her, his head tilted up, his eyebrows arched. "Sorry?"

"You said you wanted to say *again* how sorry you were for what y'all did to us."

"Yes."

"But this is the first time we've spoken since then," she says. "Again implies you've told us before."

"Oh. You're right. I guess . . . I've thought it so many times over the years and said it to others so many times that it felt like it wasn't the first time I've said it to you. But you're right. It is. I'm sorry for that too. I should've said it to you years ago. Losing my little girl has . . . I'm afraid I don't get to many things I need to anymore—including some very important ones. Please forgive me."

"There's nothing to forgive," I say. "You went through the worst experience imaginable. Still going through it. We know how much it affected us—and she was only our sister for two years. She was your little girl. Your everything. We get it."

"I appreciate you saying that, Lucas. I really do. But . . . how I failed y'all is one of the greatest regrets of my life. I've checked on y'all over the years. Kept up with you. Sent clients to you. But that wasn't enough. Not nearly enough."

I nod. Beside me, Blade begins to relax a little, to unclinch just a bit. This is the first we've ever heard of him checking on us or sending clients to us.

"I even . . ." he says. "The judge in your case was someone I knew pretty well. I spoke to him about your case, explained your situation. I hope it helped. He said it did. I think he planned to give you a much more severe sentence."

I had no idea. Tears sting my eyes and I blink several times. Clearing my throat, I say, "Thank you. I . . . really . . . appreciate that. It's . . . It means a lot."

"I've done what I could from the shadows, in the background, but it's not enough. And now y'all are here to help me. I don't deserve it. But I'm more grateful than I can tell you."

Blade says, "We're good at what we do. We're going to find out what happened. Won't stop until we do. And . . . we're doin' it for Kaylee. And for us. She was as good to us as anyone in our lives has ever been."

"She was . . . truly the kindest person I've ever known. Truly the best of us."

"Let's start there," I say. "There was a change in her—or at least in her life—shortly before she went missing. She was still kind and loving, but the wrecks and the fights—"

"There was only one fight," he says. "And she was jumped by the girlfriend of the guy Grant was fighting."

I nod. "Okay. Sure. But what do you make of what was going on with her in the months before she vanished?"

He shrugs and frowns. "I wish I knew. And I wish I had intervened. I just thought it was a mixture of growing pains—learning to use wisdom and judgement with the freedom being away at college brings—and her relationship with Grant. They were very passionate. You know how young love like that is. He was a high-strung young man. I was concerned when she started dating him, but I thought she'd have a calming and stabilizing influence on him. But now . . . I wonder how much of it was Grant at all. Seems he was in the dark as much as the rest of us. He wasn't even in the car when she had her wrecks. And she left without telling him when she drove up to North Georgia. I think they were broken up or in the process of it. He was in Miami with the music department when all this happened. And the moment he got back to UF he jumped in his car and came up and helped us search. Really impressed me. He and I . . . No one searched as much as we did. Now, it wasn't him. Something else was going on with her. I'm just not sure what. I've driven myself crazy trying to figure out what it was, but . . . I'm no closer to figuring out the truth than I was when it happened."

Blade says, "Do you think it was drugs or alcohol?"

"I thought it might be, but . . . Kaylee never drank much at all. And as far as I know never did drugs. And this isn't just a dad wanting to think the best of his daughter. I talked to her friends and to Grant. They all said she wasn't takin' anything and wasn't drinking much at all. And . . . and this is the most convincing and credible . . . she was sober during all her accidents. No DUIs."

"But," Blade says, "she . . . The night you were there y'all went to a liquor store after dinner before she and Brandi dropped you off at your hotel and went to the party. And she hit up the liquor store again before she left the day she disappeared."

"I know. All I can tell you is what they told me. She was around a lot of drinking. She even supplied some if it for their parties, but she usually didn't drink and was most often the DD."

Blade looks unconvinced.

"But don't take my word for it. Maybe they were lying to me to protect me. Ask them for yourselves."

"Oh, we will."

"I'm sure you've thought about it a lot over the years," I say, "any idea what she was doing? Why she left? Where she was headed?"

He shakes his head and frowns deeply. "Thought about little else, but I just have no idea. It makes no sense whatsoever. There are so many theories . . . and maybe one of them or some combination of them is right, but . . . I just have no idea."

"Some theorize she was running away from Grant," I say.

He nods. "I've heard that. Some writer or podcaster theorized that—with no evidence. Also said she was running away from me—from all the men in her life. He had no evidence of that. Just a throaty he thought sounded good and dramatic. But if she was running away from us . . . that doesn't explain her not telling anyone. Doesn't explain her buying the liquor. Doesn't explain why she was where she was. I truly believe that if she needed to get away from him—or anyone—she'd come home."

"Unless," Blade says, "she was tryin' to get away from you."

"Like I said . . . I'm familiar with the theory out there, but . . . she was away from me already. She was nearly four hours away. Doesn't make sense that she'd feel the need to get six hours away in the other direction. I understand why people look at the family and close friends and boyfriend of a young woman who disappears. And I know how often it's the case that they had something to do with it. But in this case . . . none of us were anywhere close to her when it happened. It's why all of us, including me and Grant, were ruled out very early in the investigation and the only people talking about it still or the true crime junkies who just like making up theories. She had no reason to run away from me or Grant or her family. No reason at all. You don't have to believe me. And you can look into it as deeply as you want, but . . . we're a good family. Loving. Supportive. We've never had any . . . There was no reason for her to run from any of us."

I nod. "We have the advantage of having lived with y'all for two years," I say. "We know what you're saying is true. What about meeting someone?"

"That one makes the most sense to me," he says, "though I have no idea who it could be. And why wouldn't they have come forward?"

"For the obvious reason," I say.

Blade adds, "They had something to do with her disappearance."

He nods again. "I guess that's true. It's also possible—maybe even likely, maybe even more likely than any other theory—that she was just getting away for a few days. Wanted to be alone. Didn't want anyone to know where she was. And . . . she gets in the accident . . . and . . . encounters someone who . . ."

He is unable to finish that thought.

15

"He could be right," Blade says.

"About the stranger abduction?" I say.

"Yeah. And if he is..."

"Then solving the mysteries of why she was acting the way she was and why she was up there and where she was headed and why she was going in the first place won't get us any closer to finding her. But if he's wrong... and what happened to her is related to why she was where she was and what she was doing... then our only hope of solving the second mystery is to solve the first."

She nods. "Much as I'd like to jump to the second... we got to work them all."

We are in a rental car on I-10 heading east toward Live Oak to pick up I-75 to Gainesville. We picked up Blaze pizza in Tallahassee and are still eating it as we talk.

"We can work the first and the second more or less simultaneously," I say.

She nods again, taking another big bite of the slice of sausage and onion in her hand.

"Or we can split up and each of us work different aspects if we need to."

"Might have to," she says. "Either for time or . . . so the camera crew don't see certain things we do."

"Yeah. We're already doing a good bit they're not seeing. Like to keep it that way as much as we can."

"Ditt-fucking-o."

While holding the wheel with my left hand, I grab another slice from the box in my lap with my right and devour it. The thin, crispy crust and the spicy tomato sauce make this one of my favorite pizzas. While I'm at it, I have another slice and chase it down with some ice-cold sweet tea.

Blade doesn't seem to mind the break in our conversation. She's working on her pizza as well. We each have our own and I'd be willing to bet there won't be any left of either of them when we're finished.

"It's odd Kay wouldn't meet with us," I say. "Wonder why after all this time—"

"Guilt. Who you know throw a bag of kittens in the river and then go back and visit them if by some miracle they survive?"

"Guess so. Seems strange, though. She could've just taken Ben's approach and apologize and explain or just not even broached the subject, but to not meet with us at all . . ."

"Maybe she got somethin' to hide."

"Hard to imagine," I say, "but maybe. Can't see that there's some big family secret. We would've seen it. Can't hide something like that for two years."

"We were kids," she says. "Could'a missed it."

"We weren't that young. And there was nothing. These are good people. We had already been around enough bad ones to know the difference."

"True."

"We'd've felt something was wrong even if we couldn't say exactly what it was. There was nothing."

"Maybe there was nothing and now there is," she says.

"Hey, if that's where the evidence leads then that's where we'll go, but not because of speculation from true crime junkies or unethical podcasters. Anyone can say anything—like Kaitlin."

"Yeah, bitch wouldn't know the truth if it jumped up and bit her tit."

"She wasn't honest about what she said and did back then and she just made shit up about Kaylee. There's no evidence she was pregnant. No evidence she was running away to start a new life. We both know how hard that is to do. What'd she have? Like six hundred bucks in cash."

"Less."

"No way she could runaway and start a new life on that. Might as well have said she ran off to join the circus. No evidence of fake birth certificate, passport, ID, credit cards. Nothing."

"She could'a had all that and a big bag o' cash," she says. "And she could'a been pregnant."

"Sure," I say, "until we know for sure . . . everything is on the table. And that's the problem. With so little to go on, so little that's known, all these true crime conspiracy theorists fill the void with soap opera shit."

"And yet . . ." she says. "Something strange went down and caused her to do what she did and vanish in the night and still be gone with no trace ten years later."

16

Gainesville seems smaller than it is. It's the most populated town in North Central Florida and houses the fourth largest public university in the country, but you wouldn't know it. It's spread out, and like Tallahassee, there's lots of greenery and trees.

We exit I-75 at Newberry Road and make our way around to the Barnes & Noble in Butler Plaza.

We're meeting Jennifer Jackson, Kaylee's supervisor, but we're a few minutes early, so I look around while Blade has a cup of coffee in the cafe.

When I join Blade and Jennifer in the cafe a little while later, I'm carrying the only Cormac McCarthy book I don't own, the new Michael Connelly, a new biography of Bob Dylan, and a book on loss called "I'm Grieving as Fast as I can."

Jackson eyes my small stack of books. "Nice selections."

She's the manager at this location. She's a thick, mid-thirties African-American woman with large hair and breasts, with a sweet, round face and huge black eyes that seem to attract all the available light.

"Would either of you like a coffee or a danish?" she asks. "I'm going to have some."

"Sure," I say. "Thanks."

She motions to one of the workers behind the counter—a young man with black hair and glasses who looks to be a college student—and he comes over to take our order.

When he leaves, she says, "I was a few years ahead of Kaylee. I went on to get a masters and started a Ph. D. Thought I wanted to teach, but . . . that wasn't for me. Happiest I've ever been is right here in this bookstore. I love to read and I love to help other readers find books they'll love. I loved reading back then too. Kaylee and I had sort of our own bookclub together. I remember we read "All the Light We Cannot See" and "Big Little Lies." We were in the middle of "The Body Keeps the Score" when she disappeared."

The young man brings our order to the table and silently places our coffee and sweets before us.

Raising her coffee cup, Jennifer says, "To Kaylee."

We tap our paper cups together and drink to Kaylee.

Jennifer's voluptuous lips have a soft, light purple lipstick on them, some of which transfers to her cup.

"I still can't believe it has been ten years and still no sign of her," she says.

"We have questions for you, but before we get to those . . . could you tell us any thoughts or theories you have about what happened?"

"I'm not sure I have any. I . . . I can tell you this. . . I was shocked she left without saying anything. We were closer than just coworkers. And she was always so thoughtful and considerate. She never once missed work before that night. She was so responsible. Such a good student. Whatever was going on . . . made her act completely out of character."

"Any idea what that was?" I ask.

She shakes her head as she takes another bite of her danish

and a few more sips of coffee. "That's what's so . . . confusing. I know a lot of people say it was Grant, but . . . he wasn't a bad guy. He wasn't as together as Kaylee. Not as kind or caring, but who was? She was an angel. Truly. She used to talk to me about him and I saw them together a good bit. He was . . . he had some typical insecurity of boys that age, but . . . I think he was scared of losing her. He knew what he had and he knew he wasn't her equal. He was tryin' to improve. He really was. I don't buy she was running from him."

"Her cousin suggested she might have been pregnant," I say.

She shakes her head. "Nope. A few months before she thought she might have been, but she wasn't."

"Had she changed in the weeks or months leading up to her disappearance?" I ask.

She shakes her head again. "No. Not really."

"But," Blade says, "she was gettin' into some trouble. Wrecks. Fights."

"She seemed just the same to me. Maybe a little more tired. Wasn't as with it, but only a little. Not sure anyone else even noticed. And it wasn't fights. It was just one. And she got jumped. All she did was defend herself. The wrecks were a little more . . . I couldn't really understand what was going on with them."

"Was she drinkin' a lot?"

"I'm not sure she was drinking at all."

"Drugs?"

"No way. Absolutely not. She never. That's why I don't have . . . an explanation."

"What about the night you found her so upset and had to take her to her room?" I say.

"Yeah, that was weird. She was just out of it . . . like . . . in a fugue state."

"You just walked in and found her like that?"

She nods. "Yeah. I asked her what was wrong, tried to talk to her, but got no response. When I got her up and was walking her to her room I asked her again. The only thing she said was Kaitlin. Nothing else. No explanation. And no matter how hard I tried I couldn't get her to say anything else. I put her to bed. Checked on her later. She was sleeping soundly."

Blade says, "You think it 'cause she hit Blake Christie with her car earlier that night?"

"I don't, but . . ."

"But?"

"I guess it's at least possible. I'm not saying it happened. Don't think it did. But . . . it could have I guess. She would often run out for food around that area. In that one block there was a pizza place, a sandwich shop, and a bodega. She was always in a hurry to get back to the desk . . . so she could've hit him. But . . . and this is the kicker . . . she's not the kind of person to leave a scene like that. Y'all know that. And she would've told me. But, hey, he survived. So y'all can talk to him."

"Anyone else you think we should talk to?"

"Her friend Brandi and her cousin Kaitlin."

"How about Andrew Collins?" Blade asks.

She nods. "Definitely. I didn't think there was anything goin' on at the time. She played it off and just said he was a flirt, but lots came out about him later. Lost his job. And that's hard to do. Definitely talk to his perv ass."

17

Andrew Collins is a phys ed teacher and girls basketball coach at a prep school north of Gainesville called Laurel Oak Academy.

As we drive back up I-75 to meet him, Blade says, "We just came from this direction. I fuckin' hate backtracking."

"I need to check in with the sheriff's department when we finish with Collins."

"Damn your criminal ass is a lot of trouble."

Ignoring her I say, "Gainesville school system must be modeled after the Catholic Church."

"How's that?"

"Collins loses his job for fuckin' the students so they just move him to another school—where they're younger and even more vulnerable."

"I say once we get the info we need, we break his dick."

The campus of Laurel Oak Academy looks more like a prestigious liberal arts college in the north east than a high school in Florida. It's exclusive and monied and very proud of it.

We find Collins sitting under an oak tree in a portable

canvas chair, watching as junior and senior girls play softball on a small, manicured field.

The sun is high in the cloudless sky and the day is bright and unseasonably warm, even for Central Florida.

He's a mid-thirties white man with thick dirty blond hair, brilliant blue eyes, and deeply tanned skin. He's wearing coaches shorts, a matching sports shirt, a windbreaker, and a visor—all in the burgundy and black of the school's colors and all bearing the school's oak tree logo.

He's drinking iced tea from a mason jar and doesn't stand when we walk up.

With the enhanced security school shootings have made necessary, I'm sure Blade and I would've had to be buzzed into the main office and required to show our ID, but we're able to walk right up to the softball field, which is in between the football and baseball fields and is just as "on-campus" as anything else.

"Don't know what I can tell y'all," Collins is saying. "I told everything I knew to the police back then and in a few interviews over the years. Got nothing new to add and it's been so long now I'm sure I've forgotten a thing or two."

"We'd appreciate it if you'd just tell us everything you remember."

"Well, Kaylee was a sweetheart. A really good, sweet girl. And she wasn't silly like so many young women. She had a good head on her shoulders. She was a good student. A good worker. A good person."

As he speaks, he watches the young women in their skin-like athletic shorts and shirts run and jump and bounce around the field.

"She never gave me one minute's problem. Wish they could all be like her. I was shocked and saddened by her disappearance."

He speaks with a heavy Southern drawl, behind which are

the desultory sounds of an aluminum bat striking a softball, the snap of leather gloves, and the yells, cheers, and giggling laughter of adolescent girls.

The large oak we're beneath provides plenty of shade and is several degrees cooler than out in the open sunlight, especially when the breeze dusts up.

"You have any idea where she was headed or why?" I ask.

He shakes his head.

"Anything she did or said in the weeks leading up to her disappearance that might give us any insight into what she was doing?"

He shakes his head again, his focus still on the action on the field. "Like I said, she was always pleasant and kind. Never saw her act any other way."

"Were you aware she had gotten into a fight and a few traffic accidents during that time?"

"She never mentioned anything like that to me."

"Did she mention her boyfriend?"

"She mentioned they broke up, I think, but . . . nothing else that I recall."

"When was that?" I ask.

He shrugs. "Shortly before she left I believe. She was probably just getting away to clear her head."

"Was she upset? Do you know what happened?"

"Not at all. She was . . . happy . . . relieved. Said she was still gonna try to be his friend and help him if she could."

"So she broke up with him?"

"Yeah."

"Did she say why?"

"Tired of his bullshit, I think. He was very dramatic. Think she'd had enough. Can't really remember many details."

"Oh, you doin' just fine," Blade says. "Seem to remember a lot about this."

"I only have a few more minutes before I have to get this class back inside and—"

"Tell us about your relationship," I say.

"What? Why? I'm married to the history teacher. We've—"

"Not your current relationship," I say. "Your relationship with Kaylee."

"I already have. I told you. She was easy to work with. Never any issues."

"I mean your personal, intimate, sexual relationship with her. You're the reason she broke up with her boyfriend, right?"

"*What? No.*"

He tries to sound shocked and outraged but can't pull it off.

"Kaylee and I didn't have a personal relationship, let alone an . . . intimate one."

"That's not what we hear," Blade says.

"Well, you hear wrong."

I say, "You lost your job for fuckin' students. We know what you are."

He turns away from the softball game for the first time and looks up at me.

"What I *am*? I'll tell you what I am. I'm a man who likes women."

"Women or girls?" Blade says.

"Women."

He stands up.

The girls on the field take notice.

"I'm a woman," Blade says. "Wanna tussle with me?"

"First of all . . ." he says, taking a step back and returning the nonchalant-nice-guy quality to his voice. "I ain't so sure you're a woman. And B I have a type and you ain't it."

"We know what your type is," I say, and turn to glance out at the girls on the softball field, who continue to play, but cast furtive glances in our direction.

"I've never once come even close to having a relationship

with any of my students here. Not once. Not close. Do I like sex? Yes. Do I like fine, fit young women? Yes. Have I ever been involved with an underage girl? Absolutely not. My wife and I have an open relationship. I'm what's known as an ethical slut. I'm open and honest, careful and safe."

Blade says, "So the ethics of your slutness prevent you from fuckin' your students here, but what about when you's at UF?"

"Do you know the age difference between me and my students when I was at UF? Between four and seven years. That's it. You sayin' it's wrong to sleep with a woman that close in age?"

"We're saying," I say, "it's unethical to sleep with people who are your students at any age. And I'm pretty sure that shit's covered in the ethical slut manual."

"I get it," he says. "Sexual harassment and all that, but that's about power. Well, guess what, I didn't have any. They had all the power. Had me strung out like a junkie."

"Again," I say, "if you'll refer to the manual. That's not the power dynamic that matters. You were their professor, their advisor. You could pass or fail them, ruin their academic career."

"But I never would."

"Not how it works."

Blade says, "You like beautiful young women. Kaylee fit that description. And you expect us to believe you—"

"I'm not sayin' *I* wasn't interested. I'm sayin' *she* wasn't. Sure, I pursued her. But she shut me down. Wouldn't cross that line."

I say, "And you, as the ethical slut you are, took *no* graciously and moved on?"

He returns to his seat and starts watching his students again.

"I always take *no* for an answer. I don't force myself on women. I don't have to."

Blade says, "Beatin' down your door, are they?"

"I do just fine."

"What was the line?" I ask.

"Huh?"

"What was the line Kaylee wouldn't cross?"

"She wouldn't cheat," he says. "She had a boyfriend."

"But you said they broke up," I say. "So what happened then?"

"Oh, I can damn sure tell you," Blade says, "the ethical slut struck again. That's what."

18

"Sorry, but I remember fuck all about it," Blake Christie is saying about getting hit by a car nearly ten years ago.

He's a lean, muscular early-thirties white man of average height with short brown hair and smallish hazel eyes. He's wearing a black, long sleeve men's quick dry cycling set and a pair of black breathable cycling shoes with bright yellow laces.

Blade says, "You about to go ridin' or you dress like that everyday?"

He smiles. "Part of the job. And it leads to tons more clothing and shoe sales."

We are standing in between racks of bicycles in his small bike shop just off campus.

The shop, which, interestingly enough is called the Hit and Run, is impressive—overstocked with every kind of bicycle imaginable—mountain, trikes, electric, tandem, road, cruiser, city, folding, adventure, touring, kid's, and on and on.

"You got any unicycles?" I ask.

He laughs. "Of course. We have every kind of bike there is."

"What's the most expensive bike you got?" Blade asks.

"S-Works Tarmac SL8."

"What it go for?"

"Fourteen."

"Hundred?" she says.

"Thousand," he says.

"The fuck? You got a bicycle up in here that goes for 14K? I've paid less for motorcycles."

Though the shop is relatively small, the various racks enable floor to ceiling displays and utilize every inch of the showroom space.

Above the aisles, bicycles hang from the ceiling, and in between and around the racks is all manner of bike parts, accessories, and gear.

There's a repair shop in the back, and the store smells of rubber, metal, and lubricating grease. An unseen sound system pipes in adventure movie soundtrack music, and the walls are filled with framed photos of Blake with local celebrity bikers.

Blake is an avid cyclist, who turned his passion for riding into a business.

Before coming to see him, we stopped by the sheriff's department so I could register, then checked into our hotel, which is walking distance from Blake's shop.

Blade says, "And you really don't remember anything at all?"

It's after hours, the shop is closed, and the three of us are standing near the center of the shop.

"I remember everything leading up to it, but nothing after that—until I woke up in the hospital several days later. I know people theorize Kaylee Walsh hit me and want me to say one way or another, but I just can't."

I start to say something but he continues.

"Seems like such a long shot," he says. "I've always wondered why anyone thinks it's even a possibility and why some people are so committed to it when there's no evidence."

Blade says, "The craziest of the true crime junkies don't let a little thing like lack of evidence get in the way of a cool theory."

"But—"

"Here's the reasons why to think it's even possible," I say. "She had been getting into some car accidents during that time. She would often quickly run out for food around that area. She did it while working so was always in a hurry. She was extremely upset afterwards. And inexplicably left town a few days later without telling anyone why or where she was going."

He nods slowly. "Guess that makes more sense."

"Were there no eyewitnesses to the accident?" I ask.

He shrugs. "Not that I know of. But I didn't know anything for a while, so . . ."

I nod.

He adds, "You could ask the investigating officer. He's a customer. I could give you his contact info. He's not a cop anymore, but I'm sure he'd be happy to talk to you."

Blade says, "Any chance it was on purpose?"

He turns to her, a startled look on his face.

She adds, "Any angry ex-lovers? Any unpaid gambling debts? Drug deals gone bad?"

He seems to think about it. "I . . . I had a bad breakup shortly before it happened, but . . . I don't think he would . . ."

"But you ain't one-hundred on it, are you?"

"It's . . . just . . . I've never—the thought never crossed my mind."

"Was your ex crazy enough, vindictive enough to do something like that?"

"I don't know."

"What's his name? Is he still around?"

"Brian. No, he transferred schools at the end of that semester."

"Probably 'cause he ran over your ass," Blade says. "Brian who?"

"Beauchamp."

We are all quiet a moment while he seems to contemplate this new possibility.

"It's funny," he says, looking out the large plate glass window in the front. "It happened right out there. I walk past the spot every day coming here and I can't remember a thing. It . . . it was a bad breakup and Bri took it hard, but . . . I can't imagine he . . . could actually run me down."

"Then," Blade says, "you either overestimate the decency or underestimate the inherent evil of crazy bitches. 'Specially exes. That's a whole other level."

19

As we're walking back to our car, my phone vibrates and I pull it out of my pocket.

It's Karen McKeithen.

I show Blade, then take the call on speaker phone.

"Hello."

"What the hell, Luc?"

"What the hell what?" I say.

"I hear you're already investigating."

I wonder how the hell she heard that.

She adds, "You're supposed to have a camera crew and a director with you. That's our agreement. That's the only way this works. And the only way we pay for the investigation."

"We're just doing a little preliminary groundwork so the shoot will go more smoothly," I lie.

"There is no *shoot*," she says. "There is no preliminary groundwork. There is a crew following you around. From the jump. On everything you do. Understand?"

"Sure. Is your crew ready?"

"Yes. Where are you?"

"Gainesville."

"*Gainesville?*" She says, her shocked voice rising a few octaves. "Gainesfuckinville?"

"Yeah," I say. "Gainesfuckinville."

"Don't fuck with me, Luc. I'll pull the plug on y'all so fast you'll—"

Blade says, "They is no pull the plug on us. We on this 'til it done."

As usual in exchanges like this, Blade's speech becomes far more street, her tone more menacing.

"You can pull your money and lose us and the family for your doc," she continues, "but that won't stop our investigation. And it'll look bad for your show when we solve this bitch. Now, our agreement is a small crew can follow us around while we investigate. That's it. They don't get in the way. They don't tell us what to do. And you don't threaten us ever again."

"Sorry if I came on too strong. I was just really surprised you're already working. I didn't mean to . . . I wasn't threatening you."

That's exactly what she was doing, but we let it go.

"We all want the same thing," I say. "To find out what happened to Kaylee."

I say this knowing what Karen really wants is to make a successful documentary. Maybe Blade's right. Maybe I am too much of a peacemaker people pleaser. But in this instance I'm not doing it to be liked by Karen or to reduce our conflict with her. I'm doing it in the service of us finding out what happened to Kaylee—because we need her resources to do that.

"We can make this work," she says. "And create a killer documentary in the process. We just have to work together. We can do that."

"Just so we clear," Blade says. "We not working together. We conducting an investigation and y'all followin' and filmin' without getting in the way or gettin' hurt or dead."

"Right. Yes. Okay. I'll scramble a crew and get them down to you inside of five hours. Text me your location and see you soon."

20

Johnny Boy's is a dive bar not far from campus. It's owned, not surprisingly, by the aforementioned Johnny Boy and it's managed by Crystal Rose.

They were both present at the party Kaylee attended the night she wrecked Ben's new car the day before she vanished. One of the prevailing theories of Kaylee's case is that something happened at that party that caused her not only to wreck Ben's car but to flee campus the following day.

We are attempting to interview Johnny Boy and Crystal Rose in Johnny's office.

I say *attempting* because we have been joined by the film crew and we're currently waiting for the camera guy to get set up.

"Nearly there," he says.

The three person crew consists of a mid-twenties Polynesian woman named Lani Lin who serves as producer-director, an early twenties white camera guy named Leaf Levine, and a thirty-something African American man named Booker Douglas on sound.

"We startin' in two minutes whether you ready or not," Blade says.

Behind his enormous desk Johnny Boy says, "We can wait for him to get it right. Want to look our best, darling."

A born salesperson and his own hype man, Johnny Boy is dramatic and ostentatious, his gravelly voice adding gravitas to everything he says. His thick, spiky hair is dyed black and his ice-blue eyes are highlighted by a hint of blue eyeliner.

"You are going to shoot some interior and exterior footage of the club, aren't you?" he says. "Some so-called B roll. Make sure you get a good shot of that glorious sign out front, won't you?"

"Okay," Blade says without asking if Leaf is set up and good to go. "We want to talk to y'all about the night of the party. But before we get to that. Any idea what was going on with Kaylee leading up to her disappearance or why she left the way she did or where she was going?"

"Yes," Johnny Boy says. "I know the answers to all those questions."

He's seated in a plush, leather high back desk chair while Crystal Rose, a pale willowy late twenties bottle blond striking the pose of a manic pixie dream girl, stands awkwardly beside him like a bird hovering above instead of on his shoulder.

I glance over at Lani Lin. She's got to think they struck documentary gold with these two.

Lani Lin's long, straight black hair, big black eyes and smooth, olive skin are striking. Her petite frame is wrapped in a bodycon dress with a Pasifika Tribal and tropical flowers pattern, the bright colors of which accentuate the dark complexion of her smooth skin.

"I know all the answers to all those questions," Johnny Boy says again, "and I've just been waiting for you to ask me. Of course, we don't know where she is or what happened to her, darling. We'd've gone and gotten her if we had."

Above him, Crystal Rose neither indicates her agreement or disagreement with what he is saying—no expression, no nod or shake of the head. No nothing.

Blade says, "Another smart ass answer like that and I'll knock your teeth out."

"No need for violence, darling. It was just my way of sayin' we don't know anything."

The desultory sounds of a dive bar occasionally drift through the closed office door, interspersed within them are the often inane sounds of college trivia night.

"Tell us about the party," she says. "What happened to Kaylee that night? Was she roofied and raped? Was there a fight? Was she assaulted? Was she pass-out drunk when y'all put her behind the wheel of her daddy's new car?"

"Nothing like that, darling. Oh, no. Nothing even close to any of that. That party like all those was pretty lame," he says. "They weren't even parties to speak of. Just gatherings. For fuck sake we were in a dorm room. There were only a few of us. We were bored out of our gourds, so we drank and gossiped. And sometimes hooked up. Stupid college kid bullshit. Nothing exciting at all."

"Who all was there? What exactly happened?"

"The usual suspects," he says. "Small, unremarkable group. The two of us. Kaylee and Brandi. A couple of others. It was very small."

"Was Grant there?"

"He never came, darling. Not that he was invited, but he woundn't've come anyway. He wasn't our sort and we weren't his."

"How was Kaylee that night?" I ask.

"Same as she always was," he says. "A little ray of fuckin' sunshine. She was always seashells and balloons, darling."

"She didn't act any different that night than any other?" I ask.

He shakes his head. "Not that I noticed. I didn't follow her around and spy on her all night, but I didn't notice anything out of the ordinary."

Blade says, "How much she drink?"

"Not a drop," he says. "As usual. She was the DD. In the end no one wound up riding with her, but she didn't know that until near the end of the party. Brandi decided to crash there—which was good. She was too wasted to walk."

"What time did she leave?" I ask.

He shrugs. "One—ish, maybe."

I look at Crystal Rose. "Got anything to contribute?"

"Yes," she says, in the soft, airy voice of a fairy.

When she doesn't say anything else, Blade says, "And what's that?"

"The truth," she says. "Something this narcissistic asshole couldn't identify with facial recognition software."

Unfazed, Johnny Boy says, "That's a tad bit harsh, isn't it, darling?"

"Not in the least," she says. "You're too self-involved . . . self . . . obsessed to have the slightest idea what's happening with anyone else."

"I don't think that's true, is it?"

"You haven't even wished me a happy birthday today."

"For fuck sake, today's your birthday? Why didn't you tell me, darling?"

"It's not. I'm just proving the point that you wouldn't know if it was."

"Well, Hell's bells, darling Rose, you might just be right. Happy early or late birthday anyway, darling."

"Thank you. Now . . . for the actual story from that night. Kaylee was off. Not so's you wouldn't recognize her, but definitely different. Johnny B's right about that she wasn't drinking, but she was sort of sad and low energy as if she had been. But she definitely hadn't. No drink. No drugs. Not for her."

"Know what was botherin' her?" Blade says.

"Not then no. But later, yes. Later when she really got upset."

"She got upset that night?" Johnny Boy asks.

"It's why she left early."

"She left early?" he says.

"What upset her?" I ask.

"She found out Grant had cheated on her—and it wasn't just a rumor. The girl he did it with was there that night and told her. Even showed her pics of them on her phone."

"I missed all that?" Johnny Boy says.

"You miss just about everything that doesn't involve you, darling."

I say, "She left right after that?"

"Pretty much," she says. "But the thing was . . . she didn't seem too upset. Not really upset at all."

21

"So," Blade says. "She finds out Grant is cheating and leaves the so-called party early."

I nod.

She and I are standing near the door of Johnny Boy's office, as the documentary crew is getting a few additional shots and comments from Johnny and Crystal.

"And," I say, "she gets into an accident, but . . . that's over an hour later. So what happened during that missing hour?"

"Would say she went to confront Grant or the other chick, but he was out of town and she was at the party."

I nod again.

Over the years, Grant has maintained media silence about Kaylee and the case. He's talked to the family and the authorities, but not the many authors, reporters, and podcasters who beg him for interviews.

"We need to have a little chat with him," Blade says.

"We will."

This close to the door we can hear what's going on out in the bar far better. At the moment the emcee is going over the trivia questions and answers. "What was the name of the Benedictine monk who invented champagne?" he asks, pauses a moment, then adds, "The answer... Dom Pérignon."

As Leaf and Booker pack up their gear, Lani drifts over to us.

"I apologize about the delay in starting the interview," she says. "It won't happen again. I've just told Leaf when we're following you two we've just got to get the shot. It doesn't have to be pretty."

She has a gentle, unassuming way about her, but there's a directness and force in her words.

"Thanks," I say. "That'll help. It was less a deal with these two attention whores, but for everyone else we need camera and sound to be so far in the background they forget they're there."

"Absolutely. We were in a hurry to get here and had to grab who we could find. Leaf is new to this style of filmmaking. He's still obsessed with the aesthetics of framing beautiful shots. He'll let that go or we'll replace him."

We nod.

Blade says, "Good. 'Cause if his little film school ass keeps us from gettin' the info we need I'm'a shove that camera up it."

Lani nods. "That's definitely a shot we don't want for this doc."

She remains calm and pleasant even in the face of Blade's hostility and threats, and I think she might just have the temperament to make this work.

She asks, "Any more interviews or investigation tonight?"

Blade shakes her head. "I'm'a find the nearest gay bar and see if I can't get laid."

"I was wondering if I could meet with y'all to catch up on what you've done so far and what we'll be doing tomorrow so I can prep. Thought we might even film a little of what you do when you're not working."

"'Less this some sort of late night Cinemax shit, you won't want to be filmin' what my freaky ass be gettin' up to tonight."

"What about you?" Lani asks. "How freaky you gettin' tonight?"

"Reading and guitar and pizza in my room," I say.

"That's my kind of freak," she says. "Mind if I join you?"

22

My room is modest but bigger than I normally get—and I get my own, as opposed to sharing with Blade.

We figured since the production company was paying we could at least have our own rooms.

I'm sitting on the end of the bed, feet on the floor, playing guitar.

Lani Lin is sitting on the small loveseat, beside her a video camera on a tripod.

Not far from me, but out of frame, is a boom mic on a stand.

Without any help from Leaf or Booker, Lani set everything up, and she did so in the most unobtrusive way imaginable.

Her only direction to me was to just do what I would do if she wasn't there.

I've done my best to forget she's there and just work on my new song.

Beside me, my phone vibrates and I look down to see it's the call I've been waiting for.

"Luc," Alana's sweet little voice says. "Where are you?"

"Gainesville. Aunt Blade and I are working on a case."

"Where is that?"

"I'm about four hours away."

"When are you comin' home?"

"Soon, I hope. I miss you so much."

"I miss you. Can you come home now?"

"I'll come home as soon as I can. Probably tomorrow night."

"I'm bored. Mommy won't play with me."

"I'll play with you as soon as I get back. What do you want to do?"

"Go to the park."

"You got it."

"And get ice cream."

"Absolutely."

"And play hide 'n seek."

"Of course."

"And have an art competition."

"Which you will win," I say.

"Because you suck at drawing."

"And because you're so good."

"Undefeated."

"That's right. And it hasn't even been close. I love you so much. Miss you so much. Give your mom a hug for me and I'll see you soon."

"Love you. Bye."

"Love you. Bye."

When I end the call and return to my guitar, Lani says, "Daughter?"

"Niece," I say. "My heart. I'd appreciate it if you wouldn't use that—or anything with her."

"Of course. I'll erase it so no one will ever see it."

"Thank you."

"It's interesting," she says.

"What's that?"

"To see you like this. Stack of books on your bedside table.

Writing songs on guitar. Expressing so much love for your niece. It's . . . given what you do . . . it's unexpected."

"Blade's the badass," I say. "I just—"

"You can tell you can handle yourself just fine."

"I've been dealing with some anger issues," I say. "So I've been trying to not handle those sides of things if I can keep from it."

"Mind if I ask you how?"

"How I'm dealing with them or—"

"Yes."

"The usual ways. Reading. Meditation. Therapy. Support groups."

"Wow. That's a lot."

"What it takes," I say. "Some of it is court ordered."

"Oh."

"Yeah. I hospitalized a pedophile predator and because of my history of violence . . . I did some time. Still on probation."

"I have to say . . . I don't think I've ever had anyone be so candid with me—in an interview or in life."

"Lots and lots and lots of bullshit in the world."

She says, "Mind if I ask . . . do you like what you do?"

"The investigative work?" I ask.

"Yes."

I nod. "I do. I love finding missing people. I'd like more time with my niece, more reading and guitar time, but . . . yeah. I like most aspects of it."

"Everything I've read and seen says you and Blade are very good at it."

I shrug. "That's probably down to persistence more than anything else. Do you like what you do?"

She nods. "I do."

"How'd you get into it?"

"I came to it from the journalism side. I still write and

report some, but mostly produce and direct. I like digging, uncovering, discovering the truth."

Before I can respond, a knock on the door announces the arrival of our pizza.

I lay my guitar down on the bed I was sitting on and we avoid the camera and audio equipment by sitting on the end of the other bed with the pizza box between us.

The pizza is from an independent place called 500 Degrees of Kevin's Bacon. We got half meat lovers for me and half Hawaiian for her.

"This is really good," she says. "Thank you. I appreciate you letting me crash."

"I'm really enjoying your company."

"I am too. Yours, I mean."

An awkward moment of intimacy passes between us. To break it, I say "What did you think of Johnny Boy and Crystal Rose? Are they as good as they seem for TV?"

"Possibly. A little eccentricity goes a long way. People like that can come across as caricatures."

"Which is what they are, isn't it?"

"Exactly. Did you believe them?"

I shrug. "Some of it. Maybe. You?"

"I find his narcissism and her observations credible."

I appreciate the succinct way she phrases her insight.

"You asked how I got into directing documentaries," she says. "What got you into investigative work?"

"Losing Kaylee," I say.

Her brow furrows and her eyes narrow. "What do you mean?"

I tell her.

"Oh, my God. I'm so sorry. I had no idea you had a connection to her. Can't believe Karen didn't tell us that. I feel so, so sad for young you and Blade—losing Kaylee, then losing everything."

Again, I appreciate the way she phrases her insight, and her genuine compassion is moving.

"I know you don't know me," she says, "but I promise you I won't let Karen exploit that."

"She already is," I say.

"Sure but I mean beyond —"

"I know. And I appreciate it."

"So having a sister go missing led you into . . . helping other families find their missing loved ones."

"It started with us trying to find her then led to helping others and now after several years we've helped a lot of other families find their loved ones—or at least what happened to them, but still haven't found out what happened to Kaylee."

"Until now."

"Definitely our best chance so far."

"I'll do all I can to help you—or at least stay out of your way."

"Do you have an opening for the film yet?"

She shakes her head. "Got a few ideas, but no winners yet. Why? You got one?"

I nod. "I've been thinking about it and I think something that really happened would make a great opening shot. Tuesday morning, April 10th. Hallway of Kaylee's dorm. The loud, incessant buzz of an alarm clock echoes through the dorm. Droning on and on, not stopping. Annoyed students in the hallway. Cut to inside Kaylee's empty dorm room. Buzzing gets louder. Push in on the alarm clock that no one is there to silence."

"I like it. A lot. Very nice. I can see it. Then we could cut to her abandoned car on the side of road. That's . . . you've really got something there. You wouldn't mind if I used that?"

"Not at all."

"Then I think I've got my opening. Now I just need you to figure out the ending for me."

23

I wake up looking forward to seeing Lani again, and realized I dreamed about her during the night.

I'm still grieving the loss of Lexi and I alternate between feeling guilty for my attraction to Lani and feeling guilty for not feeling guilty about it.

On my way down to the lobby, I start to drop by her room, but decide against it.

I'm the first one down and I look over the breakfast options, deciding against the mushy scrambled eggs and limp, greasy bacon.

The double sliding doors of the entrance open and I instinctively turn towards them.

Blade walks in, yawning into her fist.

When she sees me, she walks over.

"Any deep thoughts during the night?" she says.

"None to speak of."

"A'right. Let's see what we can turn up today. And we need to have a little come to Jesus with the crew."

"I talked to Lani about it again last night," I say. "Don't think it's going to be a problem."

"Cool. But she ain't the problem. It's ol' Booker T. and Feather Bangs. Want them to hear it from her *and* us."

Across the way, the elevator doors open and Lani steps out.

Blade heads that way and the two speak as they pass each other.

When Lani walks up I say, "Morning."

"Morning."

This morning she's wearing a casual earth tone tropical and Floral print Hawaiian Dress and a matching flowery headband.

As before, her big, bright smile is infectious, and she exudes a peaceful positivity that's both subtle and radiant.

"Looks like you slept well," I say.

"Really? I did. Good sleep and great dreams."

"I'm sure you are told this all the time, but you radiate such a positive and peaceful vibe."

"Awww, that's so sweet. Thank you."

"You seem more like a counselor or guru than a journalist and filmmaker."

"That's incredibly kind," she says. "My grandmother used to say something like that. She was so . . . She was my everything. My . . . entire family. She raised me. She was all I had. Meant everything to me. Lost her about a year ago. I noticed you had a book on grief in your room. I didn't want to pry, but . . . if you find it helpful let me know and I'll pick it up."

"I will. I can't believe you didn't ask about it. The journalist in you must have been screaming at you to do so."

She smiles and nods. "You have no idea."

"Someone I dated for a short while was killed. We weren't really even together when she died, but I'm still trying to process that aspect of the loss—and even more so the guilt I feel. She was killed by someone involved in a case we worked. If I hadn't gotten involved with her . . . she'd probably still be alive today."

"Oh, my God. I'm so, so sorry. Can't imagine how that must feel."

The elevator doors open and Leaf and Booker walk out carrying their equipment. As they head toward us, she says, "I'd love to talk to you about this more later if you like."

24

"I've taken a lot of shit from a lot of anonymous little fuckers online over the years, but I did my job."

We are interviewing Terrance Kendrick, an officer with the Florida Highway Patrol at a rest stop off of I-75 south of Gainesville.

He's a mid-thirties African-American man who's bald head gleams in the sunlight. He's tall and thick with a bit of a potbelly. He's in uniform and sitting on the hood of his patrol car.

He's a lieutenant now, but when he responded to Kaylee's single vehicle accident in her dad's car returning from the dorm room party the Saturday night before she vanished he was a young corporal.

"Must be nice to sit behind your little computer and second guess people who are actually out in the world doing something. I don't know. Seems sad and pathetic, you know?"

He has a thick Southern accent with an exaggerated drawl, making him sound more like a redneck than what he is.

He's wearing aviator sunglasses, the mirrored lenses of

which reflect everything, including me and Blade and the film crew, but Lani doesn't seem to mind.

We are to the side and back of the rest stop's main building, which houses restrooms and vending machines, in the shade of a couple of thick-bodied pines and a spreading oak tree.

In Kendrick's shades, we can see the steady stream of vehicles entering the busy rest stop.

"That's why I'm doin' this," he adds. "Set the record straight. I'm sure I'll be reprimanded for it, but I don't give a fuck. There's only so much a man can take until he has to respond."

"We're glad you are," I say. "And we really appreciate you taking the time to answer our questions."

"I hope y'all can find out what happened to her. Have always felt so bad for her and her family. Hope y'll can get her some kind of justice and them some closure."

"Gonna do our best," Blade says.

Behind us the traffic racing by on I-75 creates a whooshing breezy sound like the beach before a storm.

"Let's start with who called the accident in," I say.

"No one."

"Whatta you mean?"

"I wasn't responding to a call. I was passing by and saw her. She had hit a guardrail. I must've come up on her just after it happened because I could tell she wasn't planning on sticking around. The car was drivable and she intended to drive it up out of there as fast as she could. I hit my lights and she put the vehicle in park."

"Was there anyone else in the car?" I ask.

"No, sir. Just her."

"She seem impaired?" Blade asks.

"Not in the least. Didn't take me but a minute to know she wasn't under the influence of nothin'. But just to be thorough I gave her a field sobriety test. She passed with flying colors."

"So what caused the accident?" I ask. "Did she say?"

"She just came into the turn too fast and couldn't quite correct it. That was it. Nothing more. Nothing less. I didn't let her off 'cause she gave me head—like some of those online fucks have said. I didn't put a drunk girl back into her car and send her on her merry way. I wrote her a ticket. I did my job. By the book."

Blade says, "Any idea where she was coming from or where she was going?"

"Said she was going to a hotel less than a mile away. No idea where she was coming from."

"How'd she seem?" I ask.

"Tired. Maybe a little distracted. Maybe a little sad. And yet, sort of happy. She . . . said she hated she wrecked her dad's new car, but knew he'd be fine about it. Said he was very patient and understanding. But she didn't say a whole lot or act like much of anything. Whole thing was about as routine as you can get. But no . . . these little online true crime junkies can't have something routine. Everything has to be some sort of a conspiracy that has something to do with why she left and where she was headed. But I'm tellin' you it didn't. It was just an unfortunate accident. Got shit to do with shit."

25

It's a day of cops.

Our second interview is with Ronnie McDaniel, the investigator who worked Blake Christie's hit-and-run.

He's a fit early forties white man with thick going gray hair cut short, a dark complexion, and a movie star smile. In fact, everything about him is old Hollywood, as if he's an unfamous descendent of Carrie Grant. This effect is aided by his expensive suit and suave, confident manner.

"I thought about going the private route for a while," he is saying to me and Blade. "But the hours and the hassle and doin' it all without a badge and backup . . . Decided on an easier line of work."

His easier line of work that keeps him well tanned and in expensive suits has something to do with finance, but I'm not sure what—and probably wouldn't understand it if I were.

"I hear y'all are good at it," he says. "Hope y'all can find out what happened to Kaylee—and, hey, if you solve my hit-and-run too . . . all the better."

We are in his investment firm, third-story, corner office in downtown. He's seated behind an insanely enormous cherry desk in a large leather office chair that resembles a recliner. Sunlight streams in through the large windows behind him to backlight him with a soft gold glow.

Blade and I are seated across from him in plush leather client chairs.

The film crew is set up behind us. Because the office is so large they are a good ten feet behind us and well out of the way. Not that Ronnie minds. He seems to like the attention.

"Did you ever have any suspects in your case?" I ask.

He shakes his head. "Not really. And it wasn't for lack of trying on my part. I worked the fuck out of that case. Got all righteous and shit about it. It chapped my ass that someone would do something like that then run away. I hate a coward. Hate anyone who won't take responsibility for what they do."

"You way too pretty to be a cop," Blade says.

He flashes his flawless smile knowingly and nods. No false modesty here. "Guys in the department used to call me Hollywood."

"Plus," she adds, "the money suits you."

"I do like having it. Never dreamed it'd be so easy to make."

"You mind takin' us through the investigation," I say.

"Well, as you know the victim was no help, but even before he woke up and gave us dick, I was canvasing the area, searching for witnesses, and going through the security camera footage of the businesses in the area. Got exactly nothin'. Nobody saw shit. The people working, mostly kids from the college, were too busy. Customers were sparse or drunk. It was an odd time. Places were closing. Just weren't many people around. Best I got was some ear witnesses, but hearing a screech and then a bang and then another screech didn't give me anything to work with."

I glance at Blade.

McDaniel says, "What?"

"We thought it might have been Blake's ex, but if there was

an attempt to stop before the collision it probably wasn't on purpose."

"'Less he lost his nerve at the last second," Blade says, "and by then it was too late."

McDanile nods. "Either of those scenarios are possible. Who'd you get the ex from?"

"Blake," I say.

"Really? 'Cause he told me he couldn't think of anyone who'd run him down on purpose."

"He doesn't think it was him. We just thought it might be."

"Ah. Well, probably worth followin' up."

"Already on it, Hollywood," Blade says. "Don't worry your pretty little head about it."

He flashes her the perfect teeth again.

"Security footage was a bust too," he says. "All of them are covering the buildings, not the streets. Could see a few random tires and bumpers, but not enough to go on."

"Who reported it?"

"Couldn't tell you. Patrol handled all that. I came in later to conduct the investigation. You should talk to Brad Allen. He was the first to respond."

26

"How do y'all think it's going?" Lani asks.

The five of us—me, Blade, Lani, Booker, and Leaf—are around a long table having lunch at a sandwich shop in an old converted gas station called The Filling Station.

Blade says, "We gettin' some of the info we need directly from the sources, but most of this is background. Shit will get real when we get to North Georgia."

Leaf says to Lani, "Will we be the crew following them up there?"

She nods and gives me a quick glance and a sweet, subtle smile.

Blade says, "Y'all doin' better 'bout stayin' back out of the way, but we gotta get goin' faster."

I look at Lani. "Is there a way to decrease set up time any?"

She turns toward Leaf and Booker and gives them a questioning glance.

Booker nods.

Leaf says, "I'll do what I can. We'll sacrifice some quality, but..."

"I have a few ideas," Lani says. "Maybe we can fit in a short production meeting this afternoon or evening."

He nods.

"Just remember," she says, "we can shoot anything we need after they finish. And we'll pick up lots of stunning images along the way. I promise. I was actually thinking you could go out and shoot the city this afternoon and in the morning. I thought you could go on your own or take Book and let him grab some sound as well. You can lens anything you want to. Be your own director."

This makes him happy.

Leaf looks at Blade and then me. "What's the chance you'll actually solve this?"

"One-hundred," Blade says.

"Seems impossible," he says.

"With Christ all things are possible," she says.

He looks confused.

She flashes a smile that rivals Ronnie's. "We won't quit until we do."

He looks back and me.

I nod.

"So—"

"There is no *so*," Blade says. "There is no nothing else to say. We won't quit until we find out what happened to her."

I say, "We're that way with all our cases, but this one is personal to us, so it's even more so."

Lani says, "She said there was no *so*."

There's a mischievous twinkle in her eye and I smile at her.

"We may not find out what happened to Kaylee before the documentary airs," I say. "We may not this year or next, but we will . . . eventually."

"Hope we do before the doc comes out," he says.

"Who's we, white boy?" Blade says.

"I just meant—"

"Bruh, relax. I'm fuckin' with you."

He says, "I hope we can keep filming until you do solve it—no matter when that is."

"Remember this," I say. "We're not cops or prosecutors. We're not trying to build a case that will stand up beyond a reasonable doubt in court. That's not our job. We're out to find Kaylee."

Book says, "You think there's a chance she's still alive?"

I shake my head. "Not much of one. And if she happened to be . . . the circumstances would be such that—"

"A fate worse than death," Blade says. "For ten years."

A silence descends on the table and everyone seems to consider the weight of what has just been uttered.

Eventually, Blade says, "But, hey, maybe she's in Canada enjoying her new life."

Leaf says, "That is one of the theories, right? And there have been sightings."

"It's a type of wishful thinking that accompanies all missing persons cases," I say. "But it's less likely than any other possibility. She didn't run off to start a new life. She's not frequenting coffee shops in Quebec."

"How do you know?"

"We know," Blade says. "Wish to fuck we didn't, but we do."

Lani catches my eye and gives me an empathetic expression.

"Y'all think she hit that student?" Book asks.

"Ain't completely ruled it out yet," Blade says.

"Mind if I ask a question?" Lani says.

"Shoot," Blade says before I can respond.

"What about the possibility of the student who was hit being put under hypnosis to unlock his memory of who hit him?"

"That's a great idea," I say.

"Make for great TV too," Blade says.

A rye smile dances lightly across her lips.

"Be worth seeing if he's willing," I say, "and if we can find someone down here to do it."

"Or," Blade says, "Brad Allen can hand us the eyewitness."

27

Our day of cops continues with Brad Allen.
He was the first patrol officer to respond to the Blake Christie hit-and-run. He now works for The University of Florida Police Department.

The University of Florida Police Department, which employs over 136 sworn and support personnel has as its mission to preserve a safe, secure campus environment where diverse social, cultural and academic values are allowed to develop and prosper through a combination of reactive, proactive and educational law enforcement services.

Blade and I are meeting with him on a park bench beneath an oak tree on campus next to Liberty Pond, not far from the UF Bookstore and Welcome Center.

He only agreed to speak with us off the record and not on camera, so Leaf and Book are out shooting footage and recording sound of the locations that will be featured in the documentary, and Lani is in the campus bookstore.

Brad Allen is an older out of shape white man in his sixties. His uniform accommodates a rather large, sloping gut and a chest that seems to be caving in on itself.

"Hope y'all understand," he says, "in my position . . . I'm not far from retirement. Don't want to do anything to mess that up. And truth be told . . . even if it wasn't an issue with the department . . . I wouldn't want to be on TV."

"No, we get it," Blade says. "We don't want to neither."

"Truth is . . ." he says. "Got nothin' much to contribute. Can't imagine I can be of any help to you."

"You mind just walkin' us through what you remember of it?" I ask.

He pulls a folded piece of printer paper from his shirt pocket. After unfolding the paper, he pulls a pair of readers from the same pocket.

"I made a copy of my notes from that night," he says. "I always carry a little Lieutenant Columbo notepad in my pocket and write down everything I can think of. My scribbles can be hard to read, but . . . tryin' to decipher them is a better bet than tryin' to unlock the memories in my old brain. And far more reliable."

We nod and wait for him to read over the photo copy of his notes.

"It was an odd scene," he says, still looking down at the paper. "Didn't make sense. Where he was . . . where the victim was located . . . I'd've said a vehicle couldn't've built up enough speed to do much or any damage at all. It was at a corner at a dead end. So the vehicle that hit him had to be turning and it had to be right at the corner. That's where he was hit. That's where we found him. So the vehicle had to be going from a dead stop to accelerating in a few feet. Don't know. I just never could figure out how it happened. Also . . . don't see how nobody saw anything. It was late, places were closing. It was a slow night, but . . . nobody saw anything?"

Blade says, "How odd we talkin'? You think maybe he wasn't hit by a vehicle or his body was moved or—"

"No. Nothing like that. Every case has things that don't add up, don't quite fit, can't be explained. I'm not saying it was any more than that, but this one seemed to have more of them or they went deeper or something. I don't know. But . . . I didn't investigate it. I just responded to the initial accident."

"Is it possible it wasn't an accident?"

He shrugs. "Never thought it was anything but . . . but . . . I don't know. Told you I wouldn't be much help."

"Are you aware of the student who went missing around that time and who some believe may have been the one to hit Blake?" I say. "Kaylee Walsh."

He nods. "'Course."

"Anything back then or thinking back to it over the years make you think it could've been her?"

He shakes his head. "No. I mean, it could've been anybody, but . . . nothin' makes me think it was her."

"She was driving a 2010 Silver Toyota Corolla and here's a picture of her at the time."

I pull out a photo and show it to him.

He shakes his head again. "Didn't see her or the car."

"What about the eyewitness?" I say.

"That's strange too. He called and reported it, but wasn't there when I got there and the number he gave me was disconnected shortly after it happened. Never was able to get in touch with him and as far as I know Ronnie wasn't either."

"He reported it as a hit-and-run?"

"Just said some guy has been hit by a car and gave the name of the streets."

"Did he give a name?"

"Yeah," he says, and glances back down at the paper he's holding. "Brian . . . I can't make out the last name. Maybe . . ."

"Beauchamp," I offer.

He looks up at me. "How the hell'd you know that?"

"He's the victim's ex."

28

"So what does that mean?" Lani is asking.

I've just told her about Brian Beauchamp being the one who called the police about Blake Christie being hit by a car.

Blade has gone back to the hotel to sleep, and Lani and I are walking to a coffee place nearby.

"Could mean Kaylee didn't hit Blake," I say. "Could mean Brian did."

"Why call and report it?"

"Changed his mind. Regretted what he did. Wanted to make sure he got help. Didn't want him to die."

"But why give his name?"

I shrug. "Did it before he realized what he was doing? Figured it'd show up on the dispatcher's computer anyway? I'm not sure."

"All of that makes sense. Could be it."

When we reach the coffee shop, I open and hold the door for her.

"Thank you," she says, as she steps inside. "Someone was raised right."

She realizes what she's said and shakes her head. "Sorry."

"All good," I say. "I was raised right. Just mostly did it myself."

Espresso Yourself is an old coffee house in an old building. Everything is broken in and well worn, and the wooden floor creaks beneath our feet.

"How'd you do that?"

"By following the old Confucius quote."

"Which is?"

"'By three methods we may learn wisdom. First, by reflection, which is noblest. Second, by imitation, which is easiest. And third, by experience, which is bitterest.'"

She nods slowly and appreciatively.

We step up to the counter and look up at the large wooden menu hanging on the back wall.

When I pull out my wallet, she says, "I can put it on the company card. I have an expense account."

"Or," I say, "you could let a guy buy you a cup of coffee."

"If I do does that make this a day date?"

"I'd have to consult the manual, but it just might."

"Then by all means . . . buy a girl a cup of coffee."

After I buy her a cup of coffee, we make our way to a table in the front next to a large window where the afternoon sun is streaming in.

She's been carrying a small UF Bookstore bag since we left campus and places it on the table beside her.

"Find a treasure?" I ask.

She nods. "A collection of Rumi poems. Do you know him?"

I nod. "Love Rumi. Especially when he's translated by Coleman Barks."

"I believe that's who translated this collection," she says, reaching into the bag and withdrawing the small volume. She holds up "Rumi: The Book of Love: Poems of Ecstasy and Longing" translated by Coleman Barks.

"That's a good one," I say.

"Do you have any favorite Rumi quotes?"

"Several," I say.

"Mind sharing a few with me?"

"Let's see . . . There are so many, but here are a few . . . 'The wound is the place where the Light enters you.'"

She nods. "Ah, yes, that's a good one."

"'Lovers find secret places inside this violent world where they make transactions with beauty.'"

Her breath catches and her eyes widen. "That's . . . so beautiful and profound. I've never heard that one."

"It's . . . perfection," I say. "The two I'm most focused on and trying to practice are . . . 'Everything in the universe is within you. Ask all from yourself.' And . . . 'Your task is not to seek for love, but merely to seek and find all the barriers within yourself that you have built against it.'"

"*Yes,*" she says. "Can you imagine if we all did that?"

"I have lots of barriers," I say.

"I think we all do."

"Some of us far more than others," I say.

"You think?"

"I know. If you've never been loved how can you even—"

"You don't think you've ever been loved?"

"I'm talking about more on a foundational level. Just saying . . . if during your formative years you were rejected and abandoned by those who were supposed to love you . . . you might have more barriers than most people."

She nods slowly and holds my gaze.

"And I have been loved," I say. "Kaylee loved me. She really did. She's not the only one, but she had a lot of love to give and gave it generously. I never doubted her love."

"I'm so, so sorry. I can't even begin to imagine that kind of loss."

29

Just as the elevator doors are about to close, a thick, hairy, heavily tattooed arm reaches in and stops them, then two men step in.

The one whose arm stopped the doors is a muscle-bound merc in black paramilitary fatigues, who probably works for Gainesville's version of Blackwater. A black windbreaker conceals the weapon holstered under his left arm. Beneath his closely cropped hair and furrowed brow, his scowling eyes are mostly hidden behind dark shades.

The other guy is younger and smaller, a frat boy whose features are disproportionate and exaggerated waiting for the rest of him to fill in.

I take Lani's hand and say, "Honey, remember? We were supposed to stop by housekeeping and grab more towels."

I pull her with me toward the doors, but Blackwater turns and stands in front of them, blocking our way.

Frat Boy says, "Get the towels later. Take a ride up to your room with us first."

"But we really need those towels," I say.

Blackwater says, "Gonna need 'em to soak up blood if you don't do what we say."

His voice is low, gravely, and menacing—just like he rehearsed.

The doors close behind him.

"What floor?" Frat Boy says.

I have no weapons and no chance of keeping Lani safe without some help. My best chance is to even things up a bit with Blade. I give them her floor with the intention of taking them to her room.

After pressing the button, Frat Boy says, "Now, there's two ways this can go."

"Let me guess," I say. "One of them is the hard way."

"Yeah, and being a smart ass leads right to it. And not only will we beat the fuck out of you before putting a bullet in your brainpan, but we'll cut her little titties off and make you watch."

"Do I get a vote?" Lani asks. "'Cause I like my tits, which aren't so much little as proportionate, unlike your facial features, and I'd like them to stay right where they are."

Blackwater growls, "I really, really appreciate y'all choosing the hard way. More fun for me. Plus I make more for every body part I bring back. Double for tits."

"If mine are as small as your associate says, they probably won't fetch much."

Blackwater starts to unzip his jacket, but Frat Boy shakes his head and nods toward the security camera.

The doors open on Blade's floor and we step out of the elevator.

"Which room?" Frat Boy asks.

I give him Blade's.

We walk out of the alcove the elevators are in, around the corner, and down the empty hallway.

"Our partner is asleep in there," I say as we approach the

door. "And we'll have to wake her to get in 'cause we don't have a key."

"Then wake her up."

I bang on the door and say, "Alix. Alix. Let us in. We left our key inside. Alix."

I never call Blade by her first name.

"Alix, wake up."

The unseen elevator doors open with a ding and we all turn to see if anyone is coming down this way.

No one does.

In a few moments, the doors close and the elevator moves on.

We all return our attention to the door.

"Alix," I say, "wake up."

"Let's just do them in the stairwell," Blackwater says.

"Alix, wake up."

"*I'm awake*," she says. "*Fuck.*

She is behind Blackwater, her small .9mm pressed to the back of his head.

In one quick motion Frat Boy pulls out his gun, grabs Lani, and points the weapon at her temple.

"Let her go," Blade says, "or the local Mama's Boys Militia will be short a roid head."

"'Could care less," Frat Boy says. "He's a gun for hire. Plenty more where he came from."

"Couldn't," I say.

"Huh?"

"*Couldn't* care less. Unless you really do care and so could, in fact, care less."

Looking back at Blade, he says, "I assume y'all actually care about this bitch, so unless you want her brains scattered all over you, let him go."

"I just met the bitch," Blade says. "She means nothin' to me."

Blade glances over at me.

"I actually do care," I say. "We've spent a good bit of time together over the past couple of days and finding myself really drawn to her."

Blade shakes her head. "Can't leave you alone for a minute."

"Ah," Lani says to me. "That's so sweet. I feel the same way."

"So," Blade says, "if it was my partner with the gun to this goon's head . . . you could negotiate, but unfortunately for you, it's me, and *I* haven't spent a good bit of time with the bitch and *I'm* not finding myself drawn to her."

"So what do we do?" Frat Boy asks.

"You put your weapon down and we have a little conversation."

"Or," he says. "We—"

"Did I somehow imply there's an *or*? 'Cause there is no *or*."

"We just came to tell y'll to leave town," he says. "That's all. Let sleepin' dogs lie and leave town. That's it."

"Not cut my tits off?" Lani says.

"Not do us in the stairwell?" I add.

"That was all just to scare you. I swear."

"And obviously it worked," I say.

"Who hired you?" Blade says.

Blackwater says, "Say a fuckin' word and I'll kill you."

"I ain't gonna say shit. I swear."

The elevator doors sound again, and we turn our attention in that direction.

In a few moments an elderly couple pulling rolling luggage rounds the corner and slowly heads our way.

They stop when they see Blade's gun.

"Hey," the old man says. "What's going on here?"

"Undercover police," Blade says. "Just stay back."

"They're not cops," Blackwater says. "We need help. Call the real police."

As soon as the last word leaves his mouth, he bolts down the hallway toward the stairwell, Frat Boy following.

Blade yells after them. "We were leaving anyway. Your bitch asses didn't scare us off."

The old couple turns and heads back the way they came as quickly as they can, which, in all honesty, is not that fast.

30

"It's one in the afternoon," I say. "Kaylee is leaving her dorm."

We're in our rental car outside of what was Kaylee's dorm. I'm driving. Lani is in the seat beside me. Blade is stretched out in the backseat, asleep.

We are retracing Kaylee's movements of the day she disappeared.

Lani has a small camera and a mic, and Leaf and Book are recording from their vehicle behind us.

"Next," I say, "she drove over to the ATM off of Gator Way," and we head in that direction.

We reach the ATM at 1:13 p.m., two minutes sooner than Kaylee did. I pull up and park in front of the small enclosure that holds the ATM.

"She withdraws $680.00," I add. "Next, she drives to the liquor store on Reid Avenue."

We arrive at ABC Liquors at 1:33 p.m., a full ten minutes before Kaylee did.

"She goes in and purchases a large quantity of alcohol," I say.

We wait a few minutes. As we do, I give a quick recap of the previous few days.

"Over the preceding weekend, the following happened. Friday night Kaylee talks to her cousin Kaitlin, calls her boyfriend, Grant, officers discover Blake Christie lying in the road, the dorm supervisor, Jennifer Jackson, witnesses Kaylee's strange behavior. An upset Kaylee utters one word, *Kaitlin*. Jennifer escorts Kaylee to her dorm room. Then on Saturday, Kaylee's father, Ben, arrives to help her car shop. Kaylee calls her brother Scotty. Kaylee, Ben, and Brandi Martin have dinner together. After dinner, Kaylee, Ben, and Brandi go to a liquor store to purchase alcohol. They then drop Ben off at his hotel and use his car to attend a party at the dorm. In the early morning hours of Sunday, Kaylee crashes her Dad's new car, goes to her dad's hotel, calls Grant. Later in the day, Ben returns to PC. Then, in the early morning hours of Monday, Kaylee searches places to stay in Helen and Dahlonega, Georgia. Later in the day, she emails Grant that she doesn't feel like talking right now, but will see him when he gets back from the music competition. She then emails her professors and work supervisor to say she will be gone for a few days because of a death in the family. Then at 2:30 p.m. she attempts to call her mother, Kay, but gets no response. That leads us to where we are now."

"What about the bomb threat that canceled classes at UF that day?" Lani asks. "Any connection to Kaylee's disappearance?"

"None that we've found," I say. "But the timing is suspicious."

"They ever catch who called it in?"

I shake my head. "It could have something to do with Kaylee's disappearance . . . or . . . she could've decided to leave when she did because classes were canceled and she had extra time on her hands."

"True."

"And it's time to get on the interstate and head north."

Which is what we do next.

Once we're rolling up the road and she stops recording, I say, "Are you okay?"

"About what happened earlier?" she asks. "I'm fine. Still a little shaken up, but . . . I just tried to follow your lead and act like you did."

"You were amazing," I say. "Remained calm and —"

"Only on the outside. I do wish we could've filmed it. You and Blade were very impressive. I was surprised y'all didn't go after them or call the police or anything."

"They weren't worth chasing and the cops couldn't've done anything."

"Who you think sent them?" she says.

I shrug. "There are a few possibilities. Most likely someone we spoke to while we've been down here. My guess would be Collins."

"Who?"

"Kaylee's advisor. He's not only the most likely, but the most likely to do it like that—hire a student and a thug."

"Ah," she says, nodding. "Makes sense. But why not confront him?"

"We will, but need to know why he did it—if he did it—need to discover what he doesn't want us to. Again, if it's him."

"I keep thinking about Kaylee," she says. "Leaving like this. Was someone with her? Was she going to meet someone? Was she afraid? Running from something or someone?"

I nod. "Something powerful or dramatic had to drive her to do what she did. And after ten years we still have no idea what that was."

We're heading north on I-75, which we will be on the majority of our six hour journey. I tried to figure out a way to take a detour over and see Alana on our way up, but there was no way without defeating the purpose of following as close as possible to Kaylee's most likely route.

"Hey, Blade was bluffing, wasn't she?"

"Sorry," I say. "I was... What'd you say?"

"Blade wasn't really going to just let that guy shoot me in the head, was she?"

"I's bluffin'," Blade mutters sleepily from the backseat. "But, I's you... I'd be more concerned about what his fool ass said."

Lani turns to me. "You weren't bluffing, were you?"

I smile at her. "I was actually calling my own bluff. I told myself I was shutdown, out of commission. After everything we've been through, after what happened to Lexi... I thought I was immune from even the hint of... even the faintest form of attraction, but... It's a testament to the incredible energy you radiate that I'm so drawn to you."

"Ain't just her energy," Blade mumbles from the back. "She fine as fuck... with her hot little grown-up Moana island girl game. *Sheee-it.* Talkin' 'bout the energy she radiatin'. She radiatin' that sexy freaky smart girl let's fuck in the sand while the waves roll in on us energy. *Fuu-uck.*"

"You've given this a lot of thought," I say.

"One more thing before I go back to sleep," she says, "and this is for Skinny Moana."

"After what you just said," Lani says. "Anything."

"Watch his ass closely. Don't let him turn onto I-10. He'll be like just a quick stop to see Alana for a few minutes. We ain't got time for that right now."

I say, "There's an unaccounted hour or so. Maybe Kaylee detoured through PC and—"

"I knew you's already thinkin' 'bout that shit. Be strong. Resist that shit. FaceTime her when we get there and take her back a little souvenir, a little Rebel Flag Build a Bear or some shit."

31

"At 4:37 p.m. Kaylee calls her dorm voicemail to check her messages," I say. "We have no idea if she had any or what they were."

Lani says, "She's a little less than an hour and a half into her trip. Think she was expecting a message from someone in particular? And why not just call or text her cell?"

"Good questions," I say.

"Why Dahlonega?" she says.

She pulls out her phone and begins typing.

Reading from her phone she says, "The City of Dahlonega, the county seat of Lumpkin County, is in the foothills of the North Georgia mountains, approximately 70 miles north of Atlanta. The year-round population of Dahlonega is estimated to be 7,000 with seasonal increases that go along with being home to a major state university."

Looking up from her phone and over at me she says, "I had no idea it was so small."

I nod.

"And no one's ever found a connection she had to it—or a reason she would be traveling there?"

I shake my head.

She returns her attention to her screen and continues to read. "Incorporated on December 21, 1833, Dahlonega was the site of the first significant gold rush in the United States. Between 1838 and 1861, a U.S. Branch Mint produced the Half Eagle, Quarter Eagle, Gold Dollar, and the Three Dollar Gold coins locally. The University of North Georgia, founded in 1873 in the abandoned mint building, was the first state-supported college in Georgia to grant a degree to a woman and is now one of six senior military colleges in the U.S. with expanding undergraduate and graduate programs. Today, tourists come to shop and dine in the historic town square, learn about the city's colorful history, try their hand at gold panning, and visit the area's local wineries."

Looking up again, she says, "So it's a tourist town."

"Yep."

"What about the place she was actually found?"

"Dawson Falls," I say. "Not much to it. It's very small. We think she was just passing through it."

She pulls it up on her phone.

"Located near Dahlonega, Georgia, Dawson Falls is at the intersection of U.S. Highway 69 and State Road 71. As of the 2020 census, the population was 3,357. Best known for its unique waterfalls, it is home to a rare pair of enchanting side-by-side waterfalls. Harvel Creek tumbles over 150 feet, and Patty Creek 50 feet, to form the intriguing double falls, which spill into Dawson Creek and flow downhill into the Chattahoochee River. To reach this dazzling display, your brief (but scenic) hike begins at the visitor's center, which is right outside of Dawson Falls State Park. The paved trail will take you across a bridge over Dawson Creek and continue through the forest. You'll hear the roaring of the falls before you see the cascading water emerge through the trees."

"Small town," I say. "Small town police force."

"Always shows most in a case like this," she says. "Even the smallest departments can handle a straight forward case."

"Absolutely," I say.

"Wonder what she was thinking as she was driving along here?" she says. "Was she talking to anyone—either in the car with her or on the phone? Was she drinking?"

"It's so interesting that everyone who knew her and was around her says she didn't drink, and yet the night of the dorm party and before she left town on the day she disappeared she bought a lot of liquor. I can't reconcile those two things."

"What about the theories that someone was with her or in another vehicle behind her?"

I shrug. "Like most of the theories . . . there's not much evidence. After the accident, one of the witnesses said she saw a man smoking inside the car, but . . . she was the only witness that did. Could've been a strange reflection or optical illusion of some kind. What looked like the red glow of a cigarette could've been the red glow of a phone charger or brake lights."

"So many questions," she says.

"But you're asking the right ones," I say. "You're very good at this."

"Thanks," she says, and seems a little embarrassed.

"Did you cover crime when you were a journalist?" I ask.

She nods.

"Have you always been interested in it?"

She gives me a half shrug and a pensive look. "I grew up reading mysteries, but didn't get into true crime until I was a teenager."

Many people who aren't into true crime and get into it later often do so because because of personal experience. I wonder if that's the case with Lani. Especially since she says she was raised by her grandmother and she was all the family she had.

"Do you mind if I ask what got you into it?"

She shakes her head. "I don't mind. In fact, I appreciate it.

Most people I meet never ask me any questions. And I'm happy to talk about it sometime, but would rather not talk about it now. It would take too long, I'd get too upset, and I want to focus on Kaylee's case. But . . . my mom was murdered and my dad was convicted of it."

"Oh, my God, Lani, I'm so sorry to hear that.

32

I'm still reeling from her painful revelation. Stunned. Saddened. Overwhelmed.

"I . . . I'm just so so sorry. I understand you not wanting to talk about it right now, but anytime you are . . . just let me know."

"I will. And thank you. It happened so long ago that I'm actually more raw and in grief about losing my grandmother this past year."

I think about the calm, positive energy she radiates and I'm even more in awe.

We fall into what feels like an appropriate and comfortable silence for several miles.

Blade sits up in the backseat and says, "I'm hungry and I gotta pee. Do we need gas?"

"I was gonna wait until we're closer to see if we might find the station Kaylee used." I turn to Lani. "Her tank was nearly full when she wrecked."

"Got no problem with that plan," Blade says, "but I need a pit stop now."

"Next exit," I say.

"Hope I can last that long."

"Wonder how many times she stopped and where," Lani says. "Wonder if any of them had anything to do with what happened to her."

At the next exit, we pull into a Busy Bee Service Center.

As Blade, Leaf, and Book rush inside I take Lani by the hand, pull her toward me, and wrap her up in a huge hug.

I can feel her body relax into mine as she gives herself over to the embrace.

We hold each other for a long moment.

When we release each other, she says, "Thank you. You'll never know how healing that was and how less alone it made me feel."

We make our way inside, where we join the others in a quick pit stop, then with road sodas and snacks in hand, we're back on Kaylee's fateful route to her fatal destination.

Two hours later, we stop at the small, mom and pop gas station and convenience store that, given the fuel level in her car when she wrecked, is most likely to be the one where Kaylee stopped and filled up her car.

We fuel up beneath the flicking lights of the rusting canopy, water dripping through its many holes to splat loudly on the oil stained and pocked pavement.

From inside the car, Lani surreptitiously films the place.

Because we've heard how defensive and hostile locals can be when questioned about Kaylee's disappearance, we've decided it's best if I go into the store alone with a mic hidden beneath my shirt.

The exterior of the storefront is dim and uninviting. Its large glass windows filled with old and faded advertisements for soda, cigarettes, and beer. Next to a loud ice machine, the fan of which clangs against its cage, a leaning propane rack holds three paint-chipped bottles that appear to need retiring.

When I open the door it scrapes the floor and a small manual bell at the top of it rings.

From a stool behind the counter, a pale, skinny teenage boy looks up from his phone, gives me a slight nod, then returns his attention to his device.

I pretend to pursue the faded and dusty items on the old shelves.

The only items that appear not to have been here back when Kaylee was here are the candy, crackers, and chips.

I grab a couple of random items and a soda from an old Mr. Pibb floor display with melting ice in it, and approach the counter.

"How's it goin'?" I say, as I place the items on the glass top of the counter display, inside of which are a variety of lottery tickets.

He gives me what might be a little nod without looking up from his device.

After he finishes what he's doing on his phone, he begins to pick up each item and manually key in numbers into an old cash register. Only some of the keys beep as he presses them.

"Can you tell me where the nearest hotel is?" I ask.

"Mile or so up thataway," he says, nodding his head in the general direction of Dawson Falls. "Little place in town."

"Think we're gonna crash here tonight. What's there to do around here?"

"Nothin'," he says. "Not really. Big Jim's, I guess."

"What's that?"

"Bar."

"Anything else?"

"Pretty much it tonight. Water fall tomorrow."

"Any kind of tours or anything?"

"*Tours?*"

"Isn't this where that girl went missing?"

"Oh, yeah. No. No tours or anything."

"They never found her, did they?"

He shakes his head.

"Did she shop here?"

He shrugs.

I ask him a few more questions but get nothing else out of him.

"You got a restroom I can use?"

He nods toward the front left of the store. "Around that corner in the back."

"Thanks."

He finishes ringing up my purchases and I pay him. He neither bags my items nor offers to.

I gather the items that are bound for the first trashcan I encounter, thank him, and walk out.

Outside, I swing a left and another at the corner of the building, and follow the small, narrow cement sidewalk to the bathrooms in the back.

The doors of both small restrooms are open, the lights inside them off.

Beneath the faded sign on each door that holds the silhouette of a male and female figure someone has written the word "ONLY" with a black sharpie.

I reach into both bathrooms and, feel around for the switch, and turn on the light.

Though old and in need of cleaning, neither restroom is as filthy or disgusting as I expected them to be.

I step inside the Men's room, close the door, and look around.

I then do the same in the Women's.

In both there are suspicious holes in the sheetrock and ceiling tiles.

When I open the door to the Women's, a mammoth, big-bearded man in soiled overalls is standing there.

"The hell you doin' in the Girl's? You hidin' a pussy inside those faggoty ass skinny jeans of yours?"

"There were no paper towels in the Men's," I say, "so I checked the Women's. Are you the bathroom monitor?"

"This is my place," he says. "I monitor everything. You a cop or a reporter or one of them . . . podcasters?"

"None of the above."

"You need to go," he says.

"Plan to as soon as you stop blocking the door."

He stands aside just enough for me to squeeze by.

As I walk away, checking over my shoulder to make sure he's not coming up behind me, he says, "And don't come back, pervert."

33

"Made a new friend, I see," Blade says when I get into the car.

The big, bearded man is standing at the corner of the building staring at us.

"Just a big ol' teddy bear," I say.

I crank the car and pull out, waving to him as we pass by. Leaf and Book follow us.

"We heard everything through the mic you're wearing," Lani says.

"I's on my way to back your play when he let you walk," Blade says.

I pull out onto the empty road and head toward the crash site.

Lani says, "Do we know if he was the owner back when Kaylee was here?"

"If he's who I think he is," I say, "he was an employee when Kaylee came through."

"Wonder if she received as warm a welcome as you?" Lani says.

"I'm pretty sure there are peepholes in the bathrooms," I say.

"Maybe before we leave town I'a go back and put on a little peep show for him."

"Probably saw me looking around. Already paranoid because of the questions I asked the worker."

"He was a fount of information."

We arrive at the crash site a little after 7:30 p.m.—nearly an hour before Kaylee did.

I pull off the road onto the shoulder at roughly the spot where Kaylee's car came to rest. Behind us, Leaf and Book do the same.

"The hell she do with that extra hour?" Blade says.

To our right is a thick forest. Across the ditch, a weathered and tattered blue ribbon tied around a red maple tree flaps in the breeze.

I put the car into park and we sit for a moment.

The spot is on a curve, but a gentle and not a sharp one. Like tonight, it wasn't raining the night Kaylee wrecked.

The night is dark—just like the night Kaylee had her accident.

There is no traffic in either direction.

Across the street, set back off the road about forty yards is Hope Westmacott's small, clapboard house.

I glance over at it and see her looking at us through her kitchen window—the same window she watched Kaylee through.

Down from her place about fifty yards or so is Bruce Lewis's place.

Farther down on the same side we're on is an old wooden burned out barn.

"Was the barn burned out at the time of Kaylee's crash?" Lani asks.

I nod. "Yes, it was that way before she ever got here."

"And . . . the accident itself. Her car was on the shoulder of the road like we are, not in the ditch, right?"

I nod. "But facing the other direction."

"So she spun around?"

I nod again.

"So . . . what did she hit? I always assumed she hit a tree, but she'd've had to go down in the ditch and come up the other side to do that."

"Exactly," Blade says. "Good question."

Lani shakes her head. "It really is just mystery after mystery within other mysteries. Question after question."

I say, "Riddles, wrapped in mysteries, inside enigmas. And turtles all the way down."

We get out of the vehicle and stand on the shoulder of the highway taking it all in. In another moment Book and Leaf get out of their car and join us.

The night is quiet, the cool air crisp and a little windy, the only sounds those of branches and leaves blowing in the breeze.

This spot is on the outskirts of the small town of Dawson Falls. It's another three miles to the center of town. It's rural and desolate, surrounded by thick forests and not much else. Another vehicle has yet to pass by, and there's nothing in either direction on the highway as far as the eye can see.

I say, "At 8:27 p.m., Hope Westmacott calls 911—or has her husband do it for her—after hearing Kaylee's crash and looking out her window. A few minutes later . . . Bruce Lewis, the truck driver who lives right over there stops by to check on her. She tells him she's already called for help and doesn't need anything. He knows she's lying because there's no cell service here. Back at his place around 8:43 p.m. he calls 911. By 8:46 p.m., the first officer responds to the scene. Kaylee is not here. Her car is locked. The officer noted he believed the driver fled the scene to avoid a DUI. He also said the car had hit a tree on the driver's side, knocking the radiator into the fan and damaging the left headlight, making the vehicle inoperable."

"What tree?" Lani says. "There is no tree."

"And that car was operable also," I say. "There was a large, round crack in the windshield on the driver's side and both airbags had been deployed."

Lani says, "I just don't understand what caused the accident in the first place—especially one that caused that much damage and deployed the airbags. The crack on the windshield . . . You think she hit her head and was dazed?"

I nod. "I do, but Bruce Lewis said she seemed fine."

Blade says, "The officer also said he saw red stains that looked like red wine spilled inside and outside the car. Inside on the back seat, he found an empty beer bottle and the box of wine Kaylee had purchased. Which contradicts her not drinking."

I say, "At 8:54 p.m. a BOLO was issued for a 5 foot 7 inch female on foot. Then, by 9:50 p.m. the scene was cleared."

Lani says, "It just doesn't add up."

Blade says, "Get used to sayin' that shit a lot."

"What did she hit?" Lani asks. "How was she spun around to face the wrong way? Why wasn't she in the ditch?"

"Some armchair detectives online theorize the accident happened somewhere else, that everything that took place here was staged. But there's no evidence for that."

"They the same ones that say she livin' her best life in Canada," Blade says. "They just have fun coming up with theories. Don't care that they ain't based on anything."

"What about the other witness?" Lani asks. "The one who drove by."

"She claims she passed by the scene around 8:37 p.m. and saw a police SUV parked head-to-head with Kaylee's car. She did not see anyone inside or outside of either vehicle. It's significant because the other witnesses and the official record state that the police didn't respond until nine minutes later and in a car not an SUV. At the time, the force only had one SUV and it belonged to the chief, who was known to have a drinking problem, and was off that night."

Book says, "That sounds sus as fuck to me."

"It is," Blade says. "And get this . . . He no longer the chief. The officer that responded to the scene that night is. He became chief after arresting the other one for DUI a few years back."

I say, "There's another witness too. Just not to what was happening here. A contractor on his way home from work between 8:00 and 8:30 p.m. claimed he saw a young woman jogging east on Highway 69 about five miles away from here."

34

"Never in all my life did I think it would turn into all this," Hope Westmacott is saying.

She is a feeble, elderly woman with white hair, large glasses, and a weak voice.

We are in her kitchen. I'm at the table with her, the others, including Blade who was concerned she would scare the old white lady, are as far back as they can get in the small kitchen.

"What did you think when it first happened?" I ask.

"Just that there was an accident on the curve. Doesn't happen often, but every now and then . . . one car doesn't turn quite enough and drifts into the other lane."

Hope's kitchen, like her house, is small and dated, the decor, which was inexpensive when new, is old and worn and faded, and there's a faint smell of pee and mothballs.

"So you thought two vehicles ran into each other?" I say.

She nods her small head slowly. "But when I went to the window . . . there was only one car out there, so . . . I figured she must have hit a tree."

"So you heard the accident before you saw it?"

"I surely did. Me and my Frank were watching one of our programs."

Her Frank is her husband who passed away about five years ago.

"We were right over there on the couch," she says, nodding in the general direction of the living room. "Well, I was. He was in his La-Z-Boy. I said, 'Frank, somebody missed the curve again.' He said, 'What?' He had drifted off. I got up and came in here and looked out the window."

"And what did you see?

"A young girl. She was already out of the car. The driver's side door was open. There was a man inside the car smoking a cigarette. No one else was around."

"Which direction was the car facing?"

She points a bony, crooked finger in the general direction we had just driven from—and from which we assume Kaylee had been coming.

"She was just sort of standing there, holding her head, looked lost and confused. I yelled into Frank to call the police.- Told him what to say. In a few minutes . . . Bruce pulled up in his big rig and stopped. All I could see was his rig—and him in it. He was facing the passenger side, leaning in that direction and talking, I assume to her, through the window. A few minutes later he pulled away. He lives next door. He drove down and pulled into his side yard and parked."

"What'd you see after he left?"

"I could see the girl again."

"She was definitely there after he left?"

She nods slowly. "Yes, but the man wasn't."

"The man you saw in the car?"

"Right. When Frank went to the living room window and looked out . . . he said the car was empty and that there was a red light like from a phone charger or a check engine light. He said that's probably what I saw. And maybe I did. I don't know. I can't be sure. Later I heard there was no evidence of anyone else in the car and no sign that anyone was smoking, so . . ."

"This is all so helpful," I say. "Thank you. What'd you see next?

"Well, Frank said I'd have a better view from the living room and that I should put on my far away glasses. I didn't wear my far away glasses to watch TV. Just to drive and see things at a distance. Frank went to the bathroom. Always had the smallest bladder, that man. I went into the living room and looked for my glasses. Couldn't find them at first. Then remembered they were in my purse on the table by the front door. Went and got them. Put them on. Went to the living room window and looked out and . . . she was gone."

"What exactly did you see?"

"Nothing. I mean . . . the car door was closed. The car was dark. No more red glow. It was a dark night. Couldn't really see much of anything. There was no girl anymore. She was gone. I went back to the kitchen window and saw the same thing. Nothing. A few minutes later . . . the police pulled up."

"Did you recognize the police officer?" I ask.

She shakes her head. "Was a young man."

"Do you remember what kind of vehicle he was driving or how he parked?"

"It wasn't a car," she says. "It was one of those . . . SUV things. He pulled in nose to nose I think. Would've been behind her, but she was facing the wrong way. But . . . it was strange. I did a few things and when I returned to the window a little later it was a police car not a . . . SUV . . . and it parked on the other side of the wrecked car . . . hood to trunk. Wasn't long until the tow truck arrived. And then they were all gone and it was like nothing ever happened. Whole thing didn't last long. "

35

After several failed attempts to get Bruce Lewis to answer his door, we drive into town.

Dawson Falls is small and rustic. The business district downtown attempts but doesn't quite succeed to be quaint and charming. It's obvious the town is trying extremely hard to be a tourist destination like Helen and other towns in this region. Everything is branded with the titular waterfall, and though there's a rustic hotel, a diner, and a handful of touristy shops, it all feels fake and forced and kind of sad.

Though it's not late, all the shops and even the diner are closed.

We check into the only hotel in downtown, the Dawson Falls Inn, the same place Ben, Kay, and Scotty stayed in when they came up here looking for Kaylee.

Dawson Falls Inn has the feel of a lodge. It's mostly wooden and decorated with taxidermy, and the workers' uniforms include a plaid shirt.

We each get our own room again and this time they're all next to each other on the same wing of the first floor.

As I'm getting settled into my room, my phone vibrates. It's Blade.

"You hungry?" she says.

"I could eat."

"Other end of town there's a little area with some actual civilization. Gas stations, a few fast-food joints, a Walmart, and even a bar."

"Give me a few to call Alana and get a quick shower."

"Don't take too long. I'm hungry as hell."

Twenty minutes later, all five of us are at a table at a Waffle House on the north outskirts of town.

"Anybody else find this town sort of sad?" Lani asks.

I nod.

Blade says, "Pathetic's the word I'd'a used."

When the waitress walks up to take our order, Leaf says, "Any nightlife in this town?"

Though the excessive amount of makeup make it hard to know for sure, I'd say she's a thirty-something white woman who appears to be in her fifties, though it's possible she's actually in her fifties. She's soft and overweight and too-early old, and has short, thinning do-it-yourself dyed blond hair. In addition to the over-the-top makeup, she's wearing an extreme amount of cheap jewelry that makes tinkling and rattling noises when she moves, and an absurd amount of Dollar Store perfume that swirls around her like an unseen cloud.

"Not much," she says. "Midget's be about your best."

"*Midget's?*" Book says.

Leaf steeples his hands over his nose and mouth and in his best Stefan from SNL says, "Dawson Fall's trendiest night club is just the place to unwind and rest your chaffed legs after climbing to the top of the waterfall. It's got everything. William H. Macy, the renown blind piss artist Pee Pee La Pew, a dark room, the North Georgia all gay bear biker gang, Furries, and a midget waterfall."

Laughing, Book says, "What's a midget waterfall?"

"It's that thing . . ." Leaf says.

"That's not bad," the waitress says, "but I wouldn't do that shit in there. Might get your balls cut off."

Book says, "Are there any actual midgets at Midget's?"

She shakes her head. "No. Midget died a while back. Her nephew runs it now. What can I get y'all?"

We all order various iterations of breakfast for dinner.

When the waitress takes a few steps away and starts calling out our order, Lani says, "It was obvious someone was in that house."

"Look at us," Blade says. "Would you open up for us in the middle of the night?"

"Wonder how many of those involved will refuse to speak with us?"

"Not as many as you think," Blade says. "I can be pretty damn persuasive. But . . . brings up a good point. People up here are cagey AF. Gonna take some real finesse to get what we need. Just want to remind everybody that the investigation comes first. We've got to get what we need. Sometimes that gonna mean y'all won't. Won't get the shot or the sound or the scene that you really want. Other times y'all ain't gonna get anything at all."

Lani nods. "Absolutely. Investigation comes first. We're all clear on that. If we can't be with you during certain interviews or activities we'll interview you about it afterwards. We may even do some reenactments if we have to."

"*Yeah*," Blade says. "Now you're talkin'. *Reenactments.* Just make sure you do me right on that casting."

I say, "Think we could get Leslie Jones? She could play the part on her knees."

Book says, "How 'bout Michael B. Jordan with a wig and some fake tits?"

"Wouldn't even need the tits," Leaf says.

"Y'all tryin' to be funny," Blade says, laughing, "but both of them's a compliment. So fuck y'all."

Our drinks arrive, and not long after, our food.

We attack it like ravenous animals.

After a few minutes of eating, Lani says, "What'd y'all think about what Hope said?"

"Mostly what we expected," I say. "Gives us a better understanding of her movements and perceptions."

"Do you think there was a guy in the car smoking?"

I shrug. "I'm leaning toward no. She's the only one who saw him. Her husband said there wasn't. Bruce Lewis never mentioned anyone else. No one did. And . . . there was a lot of stuff on the passenger seat. Definitely didn't look like someone had been sitting there."

Book says, "What about the two different cop cars?"

Nodding rapidly, Blade says, "That's sus as fuck."

"I want to hear it from the other witness, but if it's true . . . it'd put the drunk ass, off duty, chief at the scene and may even mean . . . he caused the wreck."

"That'd explain a lot," Lani says. "Since we know she didn't hit a tree. And because there was a sound loud enough for Hope to hear it over her TV. And since something spun Kaylee's car around."

"Exactly," Blade says, pointing her finger at her and nodding in rhythm with her chewing. "And would explain the cover-up."

When our waitress comes back she says, "Y'all are the ones here asking questions about that girl that disappeared, aren't you?"

"How you know that?" Blade asks.

"It's a very small town—'specially when you don't count the tourists—and word travels fast. What are y'all . . . like podcasters or something?"

"We're a lot of different things," Book says. "They detectives," he adds, nodding at me and Blade. "And we documentary filmmakers."

I notice the cook over by his station, a young African-American man in his twenties, listening to what we're saying.

"Look," the waitress says. "I'm very sorry for whatever happened to that poor girl. But she wasn't from here. She was just passing through. And whatever happened to her . . . has nothing to do with us. Our little town has been through so much. Hard for us to even make a living these days. So much time has passed. Every nook and cranny of our community has been searched. She's just not here. I don't know where she is. Don't know why she was passing through our little town. But she's not here. Please leave us alone. She's not here. Her dad doesn't even come up here looking for her anymore. Plus . . . it's not safe. People get hurt. I'm sure sayin' all this is gonna cause y'all not to tip me, but . . . I had to say something."

"We're not only detectives, but Kaylee was our sister," I say. "We're here to find out what happened to her and who was responsible. Your town and any innocent person has nothing to fear from that."

Blade says, "The guilty fucks, on the other hand, have plenty to fear. They the ones hurtin' your little town. Not the victim. And not us."

"Well, I've said my piece."

"You certainly did," Blade says. "Do you feel better?"

Without another word, she rips the check from her pad and drops it on the table.

We slide out of the booth, drop money on the table, and make our way to the door.

The young cook is waiting for us in the dark corner of the parking lot and motions for us to join him.

36

"Theys some bad motherfuckers in this little town," he says.

"More since we showed up," Blade says.

Lani, Book, and Leaf are in their car. Only Blade and I are meeting with the young cook, who's name is Reggie.

"Maybe so, but . . . y'all outnumbered."

"We always outgunned and outnumbered," Blade says. "Ain't been a problem so far."

"You dealin' with crooked cops and some straight up criminals. They finally got rid of the corrupt chief. He was the worst. Bad alcoholic. Racist, misogynist, rapist. Used to pull women over and make them perform oral sex on him under threat of arrest—or even at gunpoint. Know why I cook at Waffle House? 'Cause I'm a convicted felon. Know why I'm a convicted felon? 'Cause I wasn't token enough for him. He hired me 'cause he needed a token minority on the force, but I wouldn't go along with his little criminal kingdom, so he set me up and took me out."

"You're talkin' about Alden Reynolds, the former chief?" I say.

"Yeah. The one who was chief when Kaylee Walsh went missing. He was supposed to be off that night, but his drunk, crooked ass would drive around in his police vehicle and pull over good-looking girls. Witnesses said they saw a police SUV at the scene that night. Well, there was only one and it was his. He was the only one to ever drive it."

"You sayin' he's behind what happened to Kaylee?" Blade says.

"Don't know that for a fact, but why was he there? Why didn't he stay? I ain't talkin' 'bout some big conspiracy. Could all come down to just don't question the chief. Look the other way. That's about all I was ever asked to do."

I agree with him that that's how many corruptions and cover-ups work versus a planned and well coordinated conspiracy. What comes to mind is the quote 'The only thing necessary for the triumph of evil is for good men to do nothing.' A quote usually attributed to Edmund Burke, but which is now debated.

"But he ain't chief anymore," Blade says. "So that shit caught up with him eventually."

"That's true," he says. "Colt Stevens arrested him for a DUI and he lost his job."

"Colt's the one who worked Kaylee's case," Blade says.

"He was. And he was appointed chief for a while after he busted Alden, but . . . I'm not sure how much better he was."

"*Was*?" I say. "Is he not the chief anymore?"

"Nope. Young guy from Atlanta is. Family has a cabin somewhere around here and he grew up coming to the area."

I make a note to check cabins in the area again.

"Alden is a full-time drunk and Colt works for the fire department."

I say, "Thank you for the—"

"And that's just the cop side of things. Then there's the wicked bastards hiding in the hills. We got right-wing neo-Nazi militias. We got serial rapists, predators, and abusers. Some truly evil fucks around here. One guy went around bragging about what good head Kaylee gave and how he had her chained in his basement."

"What's his name?"

"Rick Hitchens. Then you got the Jefferson Brothers. Abe and Howard. Abe turned a bloody knife into the police and claimed it was used by Howard to kill Kaylee. Then there's the Dahlonega three.

The Dahlonega three as they've come to be known are three troubled and perpetually in trouble with the law young men who didn't show up for work at the bearings factory outside of Dahlonega the night Kaylee went missing.

"Their route to work led them right past where Kaylee was that night. Lotta people 'round here think they picked her up. Jackson Hayes. He had a house back in the woods less than a mile from the crash site. He was always creepy and inappropriate with young girls. Shortly after Kaylee went missing he poured a suspicious concrete pad in his yard for no reason. And when he sold his place, the new owners allowed some forensics testing and Luminol lit up a basement closet like a CSI set. Then there's Bruce Lewis. Truck driving serial killer. Least that's what a lot of people say."

"No shortage of evil fucks," Blade says.

"And I'm'a tell you how this town works. Everybody already knows you're here and you got a target on your back. So be careful. And I'd sure as shit stay out of Midget's."

37

Midget's is a roadhouse type bar on an empty rural highway outside of town.

Beyond an uneven and pocked clay parking lot with a handful of vehicles, mostly trucks, a dilapidated and slightly leaning wooden building with unpainted plywood repairs sits beneath a stand of tall, thick-bodied Georgia pines.

"Given what we've heard about this place, I think it's best if Blade and I go in alone," I say.

Book says, "You ain't the only one who's done time and y'all ain't the only ones who know how to handle yourselves. I ain't sayin' we need to roll up in there with our film equipment, but I damn sure ain't scared to go in."

"None of us are scared to go in," Lani says. "And I think we all should. We don't have to all go in together or sit together and we don't have to be around if you talk to anyone, but I've been in far worse and more dangerous places."

Blade nods and says, "We look less threatening and more normal if we with them."

"Please be careful," I say. "Keep your wits about you and

your eyes open. Don't drink too much and drink from a bottle you see the bartender open. And don't leave it unattended. And if someone tries to start something with you don't let them. Okay?"

"Okay, Mom," Leaf says.

Blade says, "Your ass is the very one that ain't gonna survive this shit in one piece."

We split up and walk in a few moments apart—me and Blade, then Leaf and Lani, then Book.

The small bar is dark and smokey.

We pass between a couple of pool tables with dim beer branded island lights hanging above old, marred tables with worn felt.

Small cocktail tables surround a tiny dance floor and a low, compact stage that is dark and empty. An old jukebox that plays actual 45s is next to the stage playing "Against the Wind." A couple of couples—both of which are made up of older men with much younger women—are seated at the tables and an older woman dances drunkenly alone on the dance floor. A single blue light dimly illuminates the smoke-fogged dance floor.

We make our way to the bar running along the back wall.

It's a once-nice wooden bar, injured by age and abuse that appears to have been purchased used from another bar—one end looks like it was ripped off by a chainsaw to make it fit.

Blade and I take a seat at the bar, joining a handful of other patrons, most of whom are edging toward oblivion.

The bartender looks like an older, more hardened version of our Waffle House waitress.

We both order a bottle of beer.

After she delivers our cold, condensation-laced bottles and takes our money, she moves down to take the others' orders.

Lani and Leaf take their drinks to one of the tables. Book

gets a pocketful of quarters with his beer and goes over to one of the pool tables and plays alone.

"Leaf and Lani make a good-looking couple," Blade says.

"Lani would look good with anybody."

An older guy at the end of the bar orders another drink, but the bartender shakes her head. "You know what Charlie said. No more credit. I'm sorry Chief, but—"

"I used to run this fuckin' town," he says.

I raise my hand toward the bartender and say, "Put his on mine."

"You better be loaded," she says. "He never met a drink he didn't like. Goes doubly for the ones somebody else is payin' for."

"I can buy my own damn drinks," Alden says, slurring his words.

"Evidently, you can't," Blade says.

"Wasn't sayin' you couldn't," I say. "Just appreciate your service and wanted to buy you a drink. All good. No offense."

"His broke, drunk ass ain't servin' anybody but himself any more," Blade says. "Some say that all he ever did."

I had no idea she was going to take this approach, but I go with it.

He stumbles down off his barstool and sort of trips down toward us.

"Got a big fuckin' mouth, don't you?" he says to Blade as he reaches us.

"That's not all," she says.

"What? Got a big dick too?"

"Brain," she says. "Big brain."

"A big monkey . . . brain is still just a . . . monkey brain."

He's having a hard time getting his words to come out like he wants them to.

"Not just a broke ass drunk, but a racist too."

"Show some respect," I say. "He's a legend."

"Are you two together?"

"We look like we together?" Blade says.

"Ain't gonna say what you look . . . like."

"Your life's been shit since your drunk ass ran into that girl that went missing. I'd think it was from the guilt, but I know you sociopaths don't feel human emotions like guilt and shit."

"That fuckin' girl . . ." he says. "Ruined this town."

"No, you and this town killed that sweet, innocent girl."

"Oh, so I'm a mru-derer now?"

"Yeah, rummy, you're a mru-derer."

"What're you . . . one of them innner-net de-tec-tives or somethin'?"

"Or somethin'."

"Well . . . big brain, solve the fuckin' . . . case. Do what no one else has. Where is she? What happened to her?"

"You. You're what happened to her. Your drunk ass and your corrupt and inept department."

"Don't listen to her," I say. "Let's go over there away from her and have a drink."

A large, muscular white man in his thirties walks into the bar and straight over to us.

Though it's a cold night, he's wearing a t-shirt that's a size or two too small to show off what the roids and weights have wrought. The brown belt looped through his jeans holds an extra large hunting knife on one side and a holstered .45 on the other.

"Time to go, Chief," he says, turning Alden and leading him toward the door.

"Don't . . . put . . . hands . . . on me."

"Just don't want you to fall and get hurt," he says. "My job to get you home safe."

"Ain't . . . ready to . . . go . . . home."

"Then I'll take you somewhere else, but this place is crawling with reporters," he says, then turns and looks back at us. "I'll deal with you two later."

"Whenever's convenient for you," Blade says. "Just let us know."

38

Later that night, I'm sitting up in one of the two beds in my room, nodding off with my computer in my lap.

Blade and I have split up some of the various searches and follow up and factchecking that need to be done.

The TV on the dresser is on with no sound. The room is too quiet and still. And though it's a non-smoking room, the faint hint of lingering cigarette hides in the fabrics.

A soft tap at my door wakes me, and I place my computer on the bed beside me and get up. Checking the peephole and seeing that it's Lani, I pull open the security guard, unlock and open the door.

"Hey," she says. "Did I wake you?"

I stand aside, she walks in, and I close and lock the door again.

"I was just doing a little research. Can I get you anything? Perhaps an insanely expensive drink or snack from the minibar."

"I'm good, thanks. I know you've got to be exhausted. I am too, but I wanted to . . . see you and say goodnight in person."

"I'm glad you did."

She sits on the made bed across from mine, as I return to my spot next to the computer.

"What're you researching?"

"Just then I was looking at rentals in the region."

"Find anything interesting?"

I nod. "I did. UF owns a cabin not ten miles from where Kaylee wrecked. It's used as a retreat for some of the faculty and staff occasionally. But students who know about it sometimes come up for the weekend and have parties."

Her eyes widen. "That's . . . huge. Isn't it? Like highly significant."

"Could be. Or it could be a coincidence."

"If she was headed to it for a party . . . it would explain all the booze."

"Yes, it would. Maybe it was the same group that had the dorm room party the Saturday before she left. We need to check to see if any of them missed school that week."

"That's the best explanation so far of why she was up here and where she might have been going."

"And one of them could've picked her up," I say.

My phone vibrates on the bedside table.

It's Blade.

I answer.

"Open the door. I'm coming in."

I hop up and open the door for her.

"Found him," she says as she walks in. When she sees Lani, she adds, "Y'all got dressed pretty damn fast. 'Less y'all doing some teenage over the clothes shit."

"We're workin' on solving the case," Lani says.

"Day and night," I say. "Day and fuckin' night."

"And he may just have," Lani says.

"Oh, yeah?" Blade says.

"Who'd you find?" I ask.

"Brian Beauchamp," she says. "Blake Christie's ex. He's in Atlanta. Goes by Brian Meeks now."

"Nice work," I say. "Atlanta's just an hour away."

"Field trip," she says. "Pop down and have a little conversation with him."

"Or see him on the way home?"

"*Way home*?"

"So I can check in with my probation officer and see Alana."

"Oh. So tell me how your ass solved the case?"

"I didn't. But I did find a possible location where Kaylee might have been headed."

"Oh, yeah? What's that?"

I tell her.

"That's good. We need to see if Johnny Boy and Crystal Rose and Brandi Martin and any of her other party friends missed school that week."

"Good idea," I say.

Blade looks at Lani. "He already said that shit, didn't he?"

"But he didn't use their names like you did."

"Okay. I'm gonna go. Let y'all get back to that freaky over the clothes shit, but . . . trust me. Every single thing you can do is better with your clothes off."

39

"Y'all are the talk of the town," Coop is saying.

Cameron "Call me Coo" Cooper is the new, young chief of police. We are in his office—Blade and I across from his desk, the crew set up behind us.

When I checked in with him as a convicted felon this morning, he agreed to talk to us on camera.

"We make an impression," Blade says.

"You definitely do," he says. "I looked y'all up. Y'all've done some good work. I'm impressed. I hope y'all can solve this one. I really do. You'll get nothin' but cooperation from me. I'm an outsider. I wasn't here when it happened. I'm working it too. I don't care who solves it or how it gets solved. Just want it closed."

"We really appreciate that," I say. "And feel the same way."

"Where would y'all like to start?" he asks.

"Anywhere you like," I say.

"Let's start with Officer Colt Stevens," he says. "I feel like he gets a very bad rap. Unfairly so. He responded to what he believed was a single vehicle accident where most likely the driver had been drinking and fled the scene to avoid a DUI.

And ninety-nine times out of a hundred in that scenario that's exactly what it would be. And maybe this one was. There's at least some evidence that points to that being the case. The missing woman, Ms. Walsh, could've been drinking and fled the scene because of it and whatever happened to her, happened after that. It's very easy for everyone to play armchair detective Monday morning quarterback and say Colt should've done this or that, but . . . he did exactly what I or most other law enforcement officers would do. My personal opinion of Mr. Stevens is he was an honest and good police officer. Imagine what it takes to arrest your own chief for driving under the influence."

"What about that chief?" I ask. "Many people suspect that Alden Reynolds was involved somehow that night."

"He may have been, though I put very little stock in conspiracy theories," he says. "In every case like this there's a group that always cries police conspiracy or cover-up. Not sayin' that never happens, but it's a very rare thing. A group of people just can't coordinate that well and keep a secret that long. And you don't think that Officer Stevens, who arrested Chief Reynolds for DUI wouldn't've arrested him for involvement in Ms. Walsh's case had he been? That being said . . . more than one witness claims that the chief's vehicle was there that night and I'm open to him or anyone else being involved . . . as long as it's based on evidence."

"So you don't think he was involved?" I ask.

"I think it's more likely his vehicle was there than that he was. Another officer, Chuck Finely says he was driving the chief's vehicle that night because his car broke down and that he responded to the call later after finishing up a domestic disturbance he was working."

Blade says, "But the witnesses say they saw the vehicle there a lot earlier than that."

"I know. And I'm still looking into it. But . . . again . . . what's more likely? A witness got a time wrong or . . . there's a vast conspiracy involving the police?"

"What about the rumors of other people's involvement?" I say.

"Let's go through those one by one," he says. "But as we do, let me emphasize they are just rumors. So far I've found no evidence to support any of them."

"Got it," Blade says.

"So, this guy, Rick Hitchens. He's been heard to brag about having Kaylee chained in his basement. Said he took her and turned her into a sex slave and that pretty soon he'll have her trained and broken in. So, of course, he's been looked at for it. Closely. Long before I got here. And I took another hard look at him once I became chief and reopened the case. And there's no evidence that this is anything but very sick jokes in the poorest of tastes. Everyone around here who've known him his whole life says he's always been that way. That he makes the worst jokes and says the most inappropriate things, but that it's just his quirky personality and not confessions of things he's actually done."

"Did you conduct a search of his residence?" I ask.

"I did. With his permission. Didn't make me get a warrant or anything."

"And?"

"Nothing. No one was in there—in the basement or anywhere else. No sign that Kaylee or anyone else had ever been there. I'm sure he'd be willin' to answer your questions and show you around his place."

"What about the Jefferson Brothers?" I ask.

He nods and frowns. "Two troubled brothers who've lived here their whole lives. Always in conflict. Always fighting. The younger one, Abe, accused the older one, Howard, of killing Kaylee. He even turned a bloody knife into GBI. They're continually accusing each other of all manner of crimes. And sometimes they're actually guilty. But the GBI lab concluded that the only blood on the knife was animal blood. Not human. Did Howard have something to do with what happened to Kaylee? It's possible, but there's no evidence he did. And if he did . . . it had nothing to do with the knife his brother turned in."

"What about the group known as the Dahlonega three?"

"So, there's three young men—at least they were when Kaylee went missing. Like everyone they're ten years older now."

"Everyone but Kaylee," Blade says.

He nods sadly. "Yes. That's true. These three young men worked at the bearings factory outside of Dahlonega and were known to get into trouble—especially when they were together. Their commute to work would've taken them right past where Kaylee's accident was and the night she disappeared they didn't show up for work. There have been rumors swirling around about them almost since the night Kaylee went missing. Word on the street is they picked her up and took her to a party where something bad happened, but . . . there's no evidence, just accusations."

"Have they been—"

"They have refused to cooperate in any way," he says. "Refused to answer any questions. So they've not been ruled in or out. We just have nothing to go on."

Blade says, "How 'bout Jackson Hayes?"

"At the time Kaylee vanished, he had a cabin in the woods less than a mile from the crash site. Again, lots of rumors—mostly online from the so-called citizen sleuths. He did have a reputation of . . . getting involved with young girls, but always of age and he's never been in trouble with the law. He was interviewed. He permitted a search of his property. Nothing came of it."

"We understand he poured a concrete pad in his yard shortly after Kaylee went missing."

"Said he was going to put in a dog kennel, but he never did."

"We also heard that he sold the place and the new owners allowed a forensics team into the house."

"He did sell a few years back, but if a forensics team has been in that's new to me. Must have been a private lab that was privately funded. Several online true crime groups raise money for private testing. But if it happened here I'm unaware of it. Could be before my time. I'll certainly look into it. But . . . if he did something to Kaylee and or buried her in that house . . . why would he sell? And if a forensics team found anything at all . . . I feel like the whole world would know."

40

Following our interview in his office, Coop takes us to the impound yard to look at Kaylee's car.

Wrecked and partially tarped and mostly old vehicles fill an asphalt lot surrounded by an eight feet high chain-link fence with a green mesh barrier clipped to it and razor wire looping across the top.

Kaylee's car is backed into a spot along the back fence.

Blade, Coop, and I approach it, as the others record everything from several feet away.

The small silver 2010 Toyota Corolla appears to have been in a massive accident. The front bumper is on the ground, the headlights dangling down, the jumble of engine inside looking like the rotting teeth of a demented smile.

Coop says, "None of this is from the accident. It's from being moved so many times and ten years of sitting in the elements."

He opens a file folder he's holding and begins to flip through it.

Looking at one of the last objects Kaylee ever touched, her little car that took her back and forth to high school and her part-time jobs in the Panama City Mall, and then to college and back home on the occasional weekend, overwhelms me with a sense of sadness so intense I have to close my eyes and take a moment to regain my composure.

Blade pats me on the back. "Shit's gettin' to me too," she says in an emotion-hoarse voice.

When I open my eyes again, I'm struck by the round crack and the fine spiderweb-like lines spreading out from it on the middle of the windshield on the driver's side.

Though some experts claim that it's not likely, I've always believed Kaylee hit her head upon impact and in addition to being shaken and upset and having a rush of adrenaline flooding her, she was dazed and concussed.

Looking down from the windshield I focus on the front bumper.

Blade follows my gaze.

"That look like a dent in the bumper and the hood to you?" I ask.

"You mean like a possible Blake Christie imprint?"

"Yeah."

"Could be, but . . . it's in such bad damage . . . no way to tell, and even if it is . . . it could've happened in the accident up here or while being towed or in one of the impound lots over the years."

I nod and look back at the windshield. "Any way to tell if that crack was caused by something hitting the glass from the inside or outside of the windshield?"

"You thinkin' that could be an impression of Christie's head?"

"Have always thought Kaylee;s head struck it when she crashed, but . . . just wondering."

"I sure as hell can't tell, but . . . there may be somebody who can. Damn expert for everything these days. But I still think his little bitch boyfriend Brian did it."

Coop says, "I'll see if I can find someone who can tell us."

Blade and I move toward the doors of the car, her on the passenger side, me on the driver's, and lean over and look in.

Both airbags have been deployed, their remnants now looking like white parachute material spilling out of the split-open steering wheel and the cracked dashboard above the glovebox.

"So whatever she hit," Blade says, "impact was hard enough to deploy the airbags."

Coop says, "Black box report says she wasn't wearing her seat belt at the time of the accident. Y'all think she hit her head on the windshield?"

"I do," I say.

"Damn sure looks like it," Blade says. "What else that black box report say?"

"She wasn't going very fast. 48 miles per hour. She did brake. The only other thing is . . . There were seven start attempts following the accident."

Several spots within the car—the steering wheel, dashboard, gearshift, doorhandles, console, are still streaked with black powder from where the car was dusted for prints.

"Some items have been removed from the vehicle," he says. "I have a list here. I'll make you a copy. Others were left in—as you can see."

The seats and floorboard are littered with detritus of college life—fast-food bags, wrappers, cartons, containers, and cups, soda bottles, shoes, shorts, t-shirts, hoodies, makeup, textbooks, loose change, unopened mail, an orange tube of sunscreen, empty beer and wine bottles, a frisbee and Nerf football, and some of the liquor she picked up before she left Gainesville.

"Among the items in evidence," Coop says, "are printed directions to Helen and Dahlonega, a stuffed animal, miscellaneous paperwork, Puma sweatpants, a Samsung travel adapter, can of fix-a-flat, a book, a couple of scent items for the K-9 unit, a small suitcase, things like that. The car was locked and the keys missing when the first officer arrived. There was also no sign of her phone or purse or backpack—if she had one."

"She did," Blade says. "And it wasn't found in her dorm room, so she probably had it with her."

Coop says, "Everything in her vehicle is typical for a young woman in college. Nothing raises any red flags for me."

Blade says, "For those who say she came up here to kill herself or leave her life for a new one . . . several items contradict that, including her textbooks. And why email her professors with a bogus excuse if she didn't plan on going back?"

"Exactly," he says, nodding.

I say, "We also know she emailed in her homework before she left. Why do that if you don't plan on coming back."

"Also found her birth control pack. There were five pills missing."

"Which contradicts what her cousin said about her being pregnant," I say.

"Now, this is interesting . . . " he says. "They have here listed a cellophane wrapper. No explanation. No description. Could that be from a pack of cigarettes? Maybe someone was with her and Hope Westmacott really did see him smoking."

"Maybe," I say. "Or maybe it's from a pack of gum. Could you check the evidence to see what kind of wrapper it is?"

He nods. "Already on it."

Blade says, "Now let's take a look at the impact site from the accident up here."

She joins me on the driver's side and we examine the front quarter panel.

"So," Coop says, "Whatever she hit spun her around and she came to rest on the shoulder facing the wrong direction."

We both lean down and get as close as we can to the dent without touching the car.

I'm examining it for any sign of paint or anything else I can see, and I assume she's doing the same. Though I assume after ten years of being in the elements there will be nothing to see."

"No conclusion was ever reached as to what she hit," Coop says. "And nothing else was ever done with the car. No testing or anything. Printing it was about all they did."

"That look like traces of white paint to you?" I say.

Blade moves over to where I'm looking and moves in closer. "Could be but I can't tell for sure. What you thinkin'? Alden's SUV?"

I shrug. "Wonderin' if it's possible."

"Y'all think the drunk off-duty chief of police hit her and then . . . what . . . Kidnapped her and covered it up?"

"Not necessarily," Blade says. "Not all that. Just considering every possibility—something that should've been done in the first place."

41

"Are you recording this, darling? Will it be in the movie?"

Johnny Boy and Crystal Rose are in Johnny's office, him seated in his plush, leather high back desk chair behind his enormous desk, her floating over his shoulder like the awkward, willowy manic pixie dream girl she is.

Blade and I are on a video call with them from my room, and it's as if they haven't moved since we last spoke to them.

He's dressed like a 70s film version of a vampire, his thick, black, spiky hair poking out from beneath his hat, his ice-blue eyes, highlighted by a hint of blue eyeliner, only seen when he looks out above his small dark glasses.

"We have another question for you about the party," I say.

"And we'll be happy to answer it, darling," Johnny Boy says, his voice even more gravely, "but we have valuable information and we want to make sure it'll be on TV."

"You'll be on TV," Blade says. "Promise you that."

"Did Kaylee or anyone mention the cabin UF owns outside of Dahlonega, Georgia?" I ask. "Maybe meeting up there for a party?"

"No," Johnny Boy says shaking his head. "We didn't know the university had a cabin. Sounds rustic and heinous. That's not our scene."

"We did discuss it," Crystal Rose says.

Johnny Boy jerks his head around and looks up at her. "We did?"

"You didn't, but we did."

"Fuck, I miss a lot."

"Everything, in fact, that's not about you," she says.

"So nothing important, then," he says. "That's reassuring."

"We were sayin' Kaylee needed to get away—away from Grant and school and the whole scene—and someone said someone they knew had just gotten back from a party up there and it was rad. Their word, not mine."

"Did y'all go up for a party there?" I ask.

She shakes her head. "We only mentioned it in passing. Made no plans to go or anything. And then . . . she went missing and . . . I've never thought about it again."

"You didn't think about it when she went missing up near there?" Blade says.

"She didn't. She vanished somewhere near Dawson's Creek."

"Dawson's Creek is a fuckin' TV show," Johnny Boy says. "Even I know that."

"Oh. Well . . . something like that."

"Dawson Falls," I say.

"You didn't know that was close to Dahlonega?" Blade says.

She shakes her little pixie head.

"Either of you ever been to the UF cabin outside of Dahlonega?"

"Not me, darling," Johnny Boy says.

"No," Crystal Rose says.

"Who brought up the cabin that night?" I ask.

Crystal Rose shrugs and twists her lips and says, "Maybe . . . Brandi."

"If she was going there . . ." I say. "Who would she go with or meet"

"See previous answer, darling," Johnny Boy says.

"Anyone else?"

"Grant," Crystal Rose says.

"But he just cheated on her," Johnny Boy. "And wasn't even in town."

"Well, then . . . I'm . . . I don't know."

As soon as we end the video call with them, I do an audio call with Brandi and put my phone on speaker.

"Hey, Luc, I was just thinking about y'all. How's it going? Making any headway?"

"Some, yeah," I say.

"Good. That's . . . so good."

"We found out that UF has a cabin up here and that Kaylee knew about it," I say. "The students sometimes come up and use it. Do you think that's where Kaylee was headed?"

"That's . . . interesting. Hmmm. I just . . . I don't think that's where she would've been going."

"Why not?"

"Well . . ."

"She did know about it, right? You all did."

"All who?"

"Wasn't it discussed at the dorm room party y'all had the Saturday before she disappeared?"

"I had forgotten that. Yeah, seems like someone mentioned it. I wouldn't say it was discussed."

"Y'all talked about it two days before she drove up here but you don't think that's where she was going?"

"Yeah."

"Why?"

"It's not something she'd do alone. Can't see her going all the way up there by herself."

"Were you with her?" Blade asks.

"No. And thanks for letting me know I'm on speaker. I didn't go up there with her. I don't believe any one did. And I don't think she went up there by herself. And I don't appreciate being ambushed. I want to help. I do. But . . . It's like y'all think I'm a suspect or something."

"We just wonder why you wouldn't've mentioned the cabin and the conversation about it to the police."

"Why else?" she says. "Because I was with her and killed her."

42

The Dawson Fall's fire department looks like a painting created by an artist who idealizes small town life.

Shaded by huge oak trees on both sides, the bay doors of the red-brick building are open, revealing the sparkling, bright red fire engines inside the immaculate building bays.

Above us, a huge American flag on a pole on the roof of the building whips and snaps in the wind, its flag snaps clanging against the pole.

The only thing missing is a station Dalmatian and a little boy in his dad's firefighter helmet.

Blade and I are standing with Colt Stevens out in front of it.

He refused to be interviewed on camera, so the crew is back at the hotel.

Maybe it's the uniform and the fact that he's edging closer and closer to middle age, but at this point Colt looks more like a fireman than a police officer.

"Sorry about not being willing to be recorded, but . . . I just can't. Y'all can't imagine what I've been through, the things I've been accused of. Those nuts online are vicious and will believe absolutely anything—the crazier the better."

I nod. "We know—from firsthand experience."

"People always blame the police," he says. "I get that. Easier to do than accept responsibility for their actions. And it's gotten a lot worse. Seems like we got a whole generation of people whose parents never held them accountable for anything. I don't know. But I do know nobody takes responsibility for anything anymore. They just blame everyone else. But . . . when something like this happens . . . when someone vanishes and there's so many unknowns then it's not just blame the police . . . it's come up with crazy conspiracies of how they did it."

Over his shoulder, another firefighter, a much older man, lean and lanky in large boots that clomp on the polished, painted cement, strolls across the back of the firestation and disappears through a door on the opposite side.

"All I did was my job to the best of my ability with the information I had at the time," he says. "Don't want a medal for that, but also don't want to be eviscerated. That's all. That's all I'm asking. Anyway . . . I don't know an officer on the planet that wouldn't do exactly what I did. It had all the signs of being an abandoned vehicle by a driver who was attempting to avoid a DUI. That's it. Happens all the time. Still think that's what it was. Thought that's all it was at the time. Nothing else, nothing else was even suspicious. Not at first. I have been accused of cover-up and worse—of actually having something to do with Kaylee's disappearance. Like all of a sudden I'm a, what, a kidnapper and killer of young women? You know I actually thought about moving. Thought about changing my name. But then I was like they're not gonna run me out of my town. So I changed jobs. I left the police department and the way I serve my community, which I love, and I've always loved—I was born and raised here—is by working for the fire department. I still get harassed some, but it's nothing like it was."

"Very sorry for what you've been put through for just doing your job," I say.

"It's . . . I mean in comparison to whatever happen to poor Kaylee it's nothing, but . . ."

"You said you still believe it was an abandoned car by someone trying to avoid a DUI?"

"Yeah. There was a lot of alcohol in the car—some of it spilled, inside and out. I'm not even saying she was drunk. No way to know. But seems pretty obvious she was drinking or had been. And the fact that she locked the doors and took the keys and her purse and phone . . . Classic."

"You mentioned there was nothing suspicious at first. What was suspicious later?"

"Well, the way the car was and the—the position of the vehicle and what it hit. Afterwards, everybody said she hit a tree, but what tree? There was no tree—unless she somehow went over the ditch, hit a tree, spun around back over the ditch and landed back on the shoulder facing the opposite direction. And there was no signs of that, no tracks on the shoulder or in the ditch. No trees that had been hit."

"What do you think happened?" I ask.

He shrugs. "Don't know. Maybe she hit another vehicle and they didn't stop. It would've just been a slight side swipe that spun her around. Maybe they took off—or never stopped. Maybe they were drunk and didn't even know they hit her."

"Like maybe Alden Reynolds," Blade says.

"Maybe, but I'll tell you this . . . if that was the case . . . I didn't know anything about it and certainly didn't help cover it up."

"We don't believe you did," I say.

"But that don't mean other's didn't," Blade says.

"True. But I didn't. I'm the one who arrested Alden—and it wasn't because I wanted his job. It was one of the hardest things

I ever did. I've never covered up a crime for him or anyone else."

"What about Chuck Finely?"

"What about him? If he ever covered up a crime for the chief or anyone else I know nothing about it."

"Didn't he say that he was driving the chief's vehicle that night?"

He nods.

"Was he?"

"Not that I know of."

"He claimed his car broke down and he was using the chief's SUV. Any truth to that?"

"I don't know. He did come out and say that afterwards, but I have no idea whether it was true or not."

"Did he ever use the chief's vehicle?" I ask. "Did anyone?"

"No. Not that I know of."

"He also says that that night he responded to the scene after finishing up a domestic disturbance he was working."

"If he did it had to be before or after I was there 'cause I never saw him."

"What do think happened that night?" I ask.

"I don't know. I have no knowledge that anyone else doesn't, but as far as what I think . . . I think she was drinking and got into an accident. I think she panicked and locked up her car and left. The K-9 unit traced her scent about a hundred yards down the road and then it disappeared. I think she started walking and somebody came along and picked her up or she turned into the woods then to avoid being seen and something happened out there."

"Did you develop any suspects you liked for it?"

He nods. "The boys they call the Dahlonega Three and the creep who owned the cabin in the woods. Got no evidence, but . . . of the potential suspects we developed . . . those were the ones I thought were most likely to be involved. But like I say . . . I don't know and I have no evidence. If I did I would've made an arrest. I truly believe this is one of those cases that will never be solved."

43

Donovan Macomb works for the Georgia Department of Corrections.

He's a thirty-something soft, fleshy African-American man with large, bright white teeth, seen often in his frequent smiles.

His DOC uniform is ill-fitting and balloons out around his oversized belly and is damp with sweat, and his fleshy face is shaded by the brim of his DOC cap.

Macomb supervises a DOC outside work crew of non-violent, low risk inmates that mows and weed eats and cleans the roads in and around Dawson Falls.

That's what he does now. But ten years ago when Kaylee went missing he ran the prison's K-9 unit and conducted the initial search for her.

Blade and I are meeting with him on the outskirts of town, not far from the gas station we stopped at on our way in.

Blade and I have on wireless mics and the film crew is across the street from us, well out of the way.

Macomb is leaning on the DOC work van, which is hooked

to a trailer that hauls all the equipment—mowers, weed eaters, rakes, shovels, and the like.

All around us, up and down both sides of the road, inmates in uniforms are cleaning up litter and manicuring the shoulders and ditches.

"Not sure if I'm allowed to be recorded," Macomb is saying. "Can y'all make it look like I didn't know it was happening?"

"Sure, no problem," Blade says.

"I still think about that missing girl. Feel so bad for her and her family and wish I could've done more. She's the only one we never found. Most of what I did back then was searching for escaped inmates, but . . . sometimes we'd be called in for a missing person, usually kids, and we . . . found everyone . . . except the young Walsh woman."

He pauses a moment and looks down the highway on both sides to make sure all the inmates under his supervision are where they're supposed to be and doing what they're supposed to be doing.

"I'm'a be honest with you. I don't think I was very good at the K-9 job. I took good care of the animals, but . . . I didn't get much training and I aways felt sort of lost. And all those other cases I worked . . . Well, they were straight forward. I didn't really have to do much. I don't know . . . I just feel bad . . . Hate to think I'm the reason she was never found."

"You're not," I say, "but we appreciate you caring and being so candid with us."

"Now, they didn't call us in right away, so . . . a good bit of time past . . . and it had rained . . . No one gave me any input, so I picked a scent article from the vehicle . . . Later, her family said the item we had used had been a recent gift and they weren't sure she had even worn it."

"What was it?"

"University of Florida sweatshirt."

"Take us through what happened."

"I got the item . . . let the dog alert on it and . . . he seemed to pick up the scent trail right away. He followed it down the side of the road for about a hundred yards, I'd say, then the trail went cold. At the time . . . I thought it meant she must've got into a vehicle or something, but now I'm not so sure. Could've been the weather had washed it away. Could've been that we weren't even following the right scent. I don't know."

"If she had gone into the woods at that point instead of getting into a vehicle . . ."

"The dog would've turned into the woods and followed the scent. But again, only if we were on the right scent to begin with and the rain hadn't washed everything away."

44

Brian Meeks runs a successful catering company called An Artful Taste of Atlanta.

It's located on the south side of Atlanta in Decatur, but today he is catering an event in Roswell on the north side.

The event is in an old church that has been converted into a trendy event venue.

We find him downstairs in the basement with his team, which includes his husband, Joseph.

Brian and Joseph are creating centerpieces at a large round table, while other members of their team are cooking in the kitchen, unloading china and cutlery and glasses, and folding napkins.

When we approach him and tell him who we are, he says, "I'm extremely busy. You'll have to call our office and set up an appointment."

"It can't wait," Blade says.

"It certainly can," Joseph says.

"What's this about?" Brian asks.

"Blake Christie," I say.

"Who is that?" Joseph asks.

"We only need a few minutes of your time," I say.

Joseph says, "Brian, who is Blake Christie?"

"It's okay. Keep prepping. I'll explain later."

Without saying anything else, he walks toward the exit.

We follow.

He walks through the back door and is waiting for us outside near a pine tree when reach him.

"I can't believe you show up to where I'm working and— How did you even find me?"

"It's what we do," Blade says.

"Did Blake hire you to find me?"

"We're investigating the disappearance of Kaylee Walsh," I say. "We interviewed Blake and the officers involved in his hit-and-run and your name came up."

"So?"

"So why'd you change your name and go into hiding?" I say.

"I'm not in hiding. People change their name all the time. It's not a crime."

"No, but hit-and-run sure as shit is," Blade says.

"I'm aware."

"That why you ran away from Gainesville and changed your name?"

"No. I did that for personal reasons. Is that it? I need to get back to work. I have a very important event and I need to—"

"Look," I say, "if you don't want to talk to us . . . we can ask Joseph about Blake Christie and Brian Beauchamp and—"

"I'm talking to you," he says. "What else do you want to know?"

"We want to know everything," Blade says.

"I was a different person back then. That was a long time ago. I've made so many changes . . . I don't recognize that person anymore. Nobody in my life knows anything about him and I want to keep it that way, so what do you want to know."

"Take us through the night Blake got hit," I say. "Why'd you call it in but not stick around?"

"I wanted him to get the help he needed, but . . . I didn't want to . . . I was embarrassed."

"*Embarrassed*?" Blade says.

"Yeah. I'd've been mortified if Blake or anyone else found out."

"You'd've gone to jail too," I say.

"I don't think so."

"Why's that?"

"I didn't do anything illegal. I was just . . . so messed up over the breakup."

"We just established that hit-and-run is a crime," I say.

"I didn't hit Blake," he says, his voice rising in surprise. "I . . . I was . . . following him. I had been for a while. I just couldn't get over him. It was . . . I was a different person. And I was a kid."

"So you stalkin' your ex," Blade says. "*And*?"

"And I saw her hit him."

"Her who?" I ask.

"That Kaylee girl, the one who went missing. She didn't hit him hard, but she hit him. Then she drove away. I called it in so they'd get help to him as soon as possible, but I gave them a fake phone number. That's it. That's all I did. And I never followed him or anyone else again. I left town and changed my name and my life."

"And you're positive it was Kaylee Walsh that hit him?" I ask.

"Absolutely. One-hundred."

"Did his head or any part of him hit her windshield?" I ask.

"What? No. She barely touched him. She was turning. He stepped out. Tagged him with her bumper and he fell down. Would've been nothing if he hadn't hit his head on the pavement."

45

"So," Lani says, "she hit Blake in Gainesville and most likely hit her head on the windshield when she wrecked up here."

"What it looks like," I say.

The two of us are in my room.

I'm sitting at the small table with my laptop and the case files in front of me. She's on the loveseat looking at footage on her laptop.

Blade had dropped me at the hotel when we got back from Atlanta, but had not come in and had not told me where she was going. She's also not responding to my texts.

"I just don't get it," I say. "Kaylee would never hit someone with her car and not stay to help. She'd never leave town without letting anyone know. She was one of the most genuinely kind and caring and responsible people I have ever known."

"Sure sounds like alcohol or drugs," she says. "I know her friends are saying she wasn't drinking, but . . ."

"I believe them. She was so calm and stable and . . .

together. Very centered. She didn't look outside of herself for—"

And then I have a thought.

My expression must have changed or maybe I made a sound because Lani says, "What is it?"

I pull my laptop toward me and close out what's on the screen. Pulling up Google, I begin to search for a medical explanation for the symptoms Kaylee was experiencing.

"What if she was sick or getting sick?" I say. "Like the early onset of something that went undiagnosed."

She nods slowly. "That would explain so much."

We both search for several minutes.

"Finding anything?" she asks eventually.

I nod. "Think I found it. Or at least a very good possibility. No way to know for sure, but . . . this sure fits."

"What is it?"

"Conversion Disease."

"What is that?'

"Well, I guess it's a disorder not a disease, but it's . . . 'a condition where a mental health issue disrupts how the brain works, causing physical symptoms the person can't control. Seizures, weakness or paralysis, or reduced input from one or more senses such as sight or sound can be part of it. This condition is often treatable through various types of therapy. Functional neurological symptom disorder as it's also known is when the brain converts the effects of a mental health issue into disruptions of your brain or nervous system. The symptoms are real but don't match up with recognized brain-related conditions. It's important to know that conversion disorder is a real mental health condition. It's not faking or attention-seeking. It isn't just something in a person's head or that they've imagined. While it's a mental health condition, the physical symptoms are still real. A person with conversion disorder can't control the symptoms just by trying or thinking about them.'"

"Wow," Lani says. "That fits, doesn't it?"

"I'm sure we could find a lot of diseases and disorders that would fit, and we have no way of verifying it, but, yeah, it fits."

"Whether it's this specific disorder or a similar one . . ." she says, "I think there's a good chance she was dealing with something like it."

A knock on the door is followed by Blade saying, "Let me in. I got news."

When she comes in and sees Lani she says, "Y'all always together, but I never catch you naked."

"We're getting to know each other," Lani says. "Letting things unfold slowly. It's sweet."

"May be sweet," Blade says, "but ain't nearly as fun."

"Where have you been?" I ask.

"Out."

"You have news," I say.

"Yeah. Talked Scotty into coming up and bringing his folks *and* Grant. Tol' them we need them for the documentary and for them to take us through what happened when they came up to search for Kaylee. Be good to have them all up here. Still want to know why Kay is avoiding us."

I nod. "Good work. Be nice to have Mandi and Collins and some of the others up here too. We could use the documentary as an excuse. Might work."

"I can work on that," Lani says. "And pay for their travel and lodging out of the production budget."

"God, I love TV money," Blade says. "Wish we could have it for every case."

Lani says, "I'll work on that too."

"Cool," she says, and turns to leave.

"You're not going to tell her about your theory?" Lani says.

"I was about to."

Blade turns around. "Got a unifying theory of everything?"

I shake my head. "Nothing like that. But I do have some

thoughts and a possible theory on what was going on with Kaylee leading up to her disappearance."

"What's that?"

I tell her.

After I do, Lani reads some of the information and description of the disorder.

Blade nods and says. "Would explain so many things."

"And that plus the the concussion from hitting her head on the windshield left her extremely vulnerable for whatever predator she encountered."

"A predator," Blade says, "that real soon gonna know what it's like to be the prey."

46

Downtown Dawson Falls is cool and quiet and picturesque.

The closed shops are lit with soft lights inside and appear far more attractive than they do during the day.

The streetlamps offer a soft, diffused glow, and the canopied branches of the trees are wrapped with small string lights.

Lani and I are walking back to the hotel from the small diner, after having shared a late-night snack.

"I meant what I said to Blade," she says. "I'm enjoying our time together and getting to know each other before getting sexual—if we do. Don't mean to presume."

"I am too," I say. "I'm not presuming anything either. I'm very attracted to you, but I'm also grieving the loss of Lexi and working to get my shit together."

"I so appreciate that you're allowing time for both of those thi—"

"You the one lookin' for me?" a voice says behind us.

The voice is a mixture of menace and amusement.

I turn around and step in front of Lani.

The figure approaching us is a gaunt, late fifties white man who does all his shopping at the Army Navy Store. Beneath the shaggy hair spilling out of his digital camo tactical cap, his face is pale, the skin stretched like parchment across the skull. His scraggily and patchy beard extends all the way down his skinny neck. His army combat uniform jacket is unbuttoned and if it's concealing a weapon it's likely under his arm or at the small of his back.

"Depends," I say. "Who are you?"

"I'm the one who has Kaylee Walsh chained up in my basement."

"Then I'm definitely looking for you," I say. "Rick Hitchens, right?"

"I see my reputation proceeds me."

Turning slightly toward Lani behind me without taking my eyes off Hitchens, I say, "Go back to the hotel and wait for me there. Let Blade know where I am."

She gives me a quick nod, touches my back, and starts walking.

"I's hopin' to get to know her too," he says. "She's a peach, isn't she? What is she Hawaiian or something?"

"Or something. Could you take me to see Kaylee? Where is your basement?"

"I should've said I'm the man who teases about having Kaylee in my basement. Truth is . . . I don't have a basement."

"So you really don't have her?"

"Nah. I just joked about it a little ways back and everyone lost their damn minds. Have you noticed how sensitive everybody is these days? It's like nobody can take a joke anymore."

"It's a pretty insensitive and inappropriate joke," I say.

"Exactly. The best kind. Least they're my favorite—and the kind I'm always tellin'."

"So it was all just a joke?" I ask.

He nods. "Uh huh."

"You have no knowledge of what happened to Kaylee or who might have been involved, or where she might be?"

"I hear stories like everybody else. But got no direct knowledge, no."

"Mind tellin' me what you've heard?"

"What's it worth to you?"

"Second hand stories? Not too much."

"How 'bout some time alone with that Hawaiian girl?"

"That would be up to her, not me, but I feel safe in saying her answer wouldn't be no, but *fuck no!*"

"How 'bout you?"

"We're spending time alone right now," I say.

"Let's go to my truck," he says. "Go down on me and I'll tell you everything."

When I start to say something, he holds his hands up and says, "I'm joking. Kaylee meets all my needs. Again, just kidding. Havin' a little laugh. It's a personality disorder. I'm getting injections for it."

"They don't seem to be working."

"Nothin' works, man. Everything's fucked. Always was, just it's more obvious now. People finally gettin' hip to it."

"I'm guessing you live off the grid," I say.

He nods. "Just me and Kaylee, Jasper the dog, and Fido the cat. A nation unto ourselves."

"So you gonna tell me what you've heard or not?"

"The one thing I heard more than anything else . . . is that there was a party. And Kaylee was there. Something bad happened and she didn't make it. Don't know how she got there or who else was there or what happened, but I've heard it enough that I think there might be something to it."

"Where was the party?"

He shrugs. "Don't know. Some house. A cabin in the woods. At one of the waterfalls. Those kinds of things change, but the core story stays the same. I mean . . . how many times can you hear that Richard Gere gerbil story and not believe there's some truth to it?"

47

Blade and Lani come rushing up as I'm walking back to the hotel.

"What happened?" Lani asks. "Are you okay?"

I nod. "We just had a little chat. He's an interesting character."

"Lots of those up here," Blade says. "What'd he say?"

They turn and we begin to walk back toward the hotel together.

"Says he's just joking when he says he has Kaylee in his basement, that people these days are too sensitive and can't take a joke."

"Ain't wrong about that," Blade says.

"Says he doesn't even have a basement."

"Whatcha think?" Blade asks.

"Think he's worth lookin' into. Could be saying what he says to hide the fact that he really has her. I don't think he does, but . . . we have to know for sure."

"Don't have the manpower to follow him," Blade says.

"We'll start with his house," I say. "If we can find it. He lives off the grid."

"'Course he does."

"Show up at his house unannounced," I say. "See how he reacts. See if he'll let us look around. See if he warrants a closer look. Hire back up to help us follow him if need be."

"Sounds like a plan. He say anything else?"

"Yeah. He requested some alone time with Lani."

"You tell him I was smitten with you?" Lani asks.

"He indicated he might be too."

"*Smitten with you?*"

"Yeah."

"Dude's all over the place."

I say, "Seemed to be workin' pretty hard to prove he'll say anything and that he meant nothing."

"Definitely warrants a closer look," Blade says. "Something ain't right with him if he didn't mention jonesin' for alone time with me."

"Only thing useful he said was that of all the persistent rumors he's heard over the years the only one he puts any stock in is that there was a party, Kaylee went to it, and something bad happened to her. Mentioned it being in a house, a cabin in the woods, or at one of the waterfalls."

Blade nods.

"Y'all've heard that one before?" Lani asks.

We nod.

"So," Lani says. "She wrecks her car, hits her head, is already dealing with the conversion disorder stuff, might be inebriated. She's dazed, confused . . ."

I say, "She locks her car and starts walking and gets about a hundred yards—if the scent dogs were on the right trail."

"And," she says, "somebody stops and picks her up and at some point takes her to a party."

"That'd fit more with the Dahlonega Three fuckers than anyone else," Blade says.

48

"I feel responsible for what happened to Kaylee," Grant St. James is saying.

It's the next morning and we're interviewing him in the small, empty, nondescript, intentionally neutral hotel meeting room.

Blade and I are at a table with him, the others behind us, filming.

He has come to town at the request of the Walshes and to participate in the documentary. He arrived in the middle of night and was waiting for us in the lobby first thing this morning.

"Not in the way many of the online true crime people think. I didn't have anything to do with what actually happened to her—whatever that was. I was at a fine arts competition in Miami when she went missing. But I . . . I should've been a better boyfriend, a better friend. Hell, a better person. I was young and insecure and stupid. I was so self-involved I didn't pay close enough attention to what was going on with her. Honestly, I don't even recognize that kid anymore. Can't believe it was really me."

Grant is not what I expected. He's warm, humble, and sincere. In his early thirties, he seems if not looks older. He's got a calm, self-contained wisdom that if it comes at all typically comes later in life.

He looks more like a realtor or banker or a high school football coach than a musician. He's tall and thickish, large and a little soft without being fat. His dark blond hair is cut short, parted on the side, and combed over. His face is clean shaven, and his blue eyes clear and wide with the hint of an indefinable something that might be called sparkle.

"Tell us about the fine arts competition," I say.

"I was at UF on a music scholarship. There was an annual competition in Miami we always participated in. I competed in classical guitar. We drove down on the Thursday before the Monday she went missing. We were traveling back when I got the call from her brother that she was missing. The police cleared me because there were hundreds of witnesses. She wasn't talking to me much that weekend. Wouldn't text me back. Later I found out why."

"Why?" I ask.

"She found out I had slept with another girl. I mean, I think there was something wrong before that . . . 'cause that wasn't until Saturday night—that she found out, I mean. And she wasn't talkin' to me before that. But I'm sure that upset her even more and had something to do with why she did what she did and what she was doing up here. That's why I feel responsible. It's my fault. And I've regretted it every day of my life since then."

"What'd you do when you found out she was missing?"

"Scott said they were driving up here to look for her. I told him I'd join them and help. As soon as we got back to Gainesville . . . I got in my car and drove up here. Didn't even go into my dorm. We stayed in this same shitty motel."

"Did you and Kaylee fight much?"

"We argued a good bit—the way some unhealthy young couples can do—but we never fought. I never put my hands on her—if that's what you're askin'?"

"Had you ever cheated before?"

He shakes his head. "No."

"Had she?"

"No, but . . ."

"But what?"

"We weren't . . . I swear I'm not saying this to try to make myself to be . . . I've already said I was wrong and I'm responsible, but . . . we weren't exclusive. I'm not sayin' we . . . We just hadn't really had *the talk* yet. And the only reason I bring it up is if she had slept with someone else . . . it wouldn't have been cheating."

"Did you talk or text any that weekend or the Monday she drove up here?"

"I tried to call her a few times. Wanted to tell her how the competition was going. I won that year. Wanted to see how she was. Was worried about her. But she didn't answer my calls. Didn't call me back. And texted very little."

"Why were you worried about her?"

"The way she was acting that weekend. I guess I was worried she was going to find out about Brandi."

"*Brandi?*" Blade says.

"You slept with her friend, Brandi?" I ask.

"No wonder bitch had to find her own ride home after the dorm party that Saturday night," Blade says.

"I know. It's . . . it's worse than just sleeping with someone else. I slept with her friend. Y'all didn't know? I thought everyone knew. See why I feel so guilty? But it wasn't just that. Wasn't that I was afraid of her finding out and that she wasn't communicating with me that weekend. It's how she was acting leading up to it. She hadn't been herself for a while. She was still sweet, still . . . so kind, but . . . I don't know. Not sure what it was, but she was having some issues. I thought she might have been taking something, but she said she wasn't and I never saw her drink or take anything."

I glance over at Blade and she nods.

"What?" Grant asks.

"Tell us what happened when you got up here and when was that?"

"Tuesday afternoon. Ben, Kay, and Scott were already here. You two didn't come with them, did you?"

I shake my head.

"The cops gave us the runaround. Weren't helpful. Weren't even professional. Didn't even want us looking for her. Ben and I said fuck that and started searching in the woods from where her car was found—he went south, following the river and back toward the creepy gas station where we think she stopped. I went north toward town. We stayed out so long, walked so far. I was exhausted. Walking through the woods is a lot harder than I realized and I wasn't dressed for it. Had the wrong shoes. We knocked on doors, asking if anyone had seen anything. Turned up exactly nothing. And this town, man. It was like everybody resented us being here. Some were actually hostile. Like they blamed Kaylee and us and would do anything to protect the town and its reputation. I don't know. It was weird. This is my first time back since then. I . . . I don't like admitting this, but . . . and it's not so much now that I'm older, but back then, as that young college kid . . . I was . . . scared. This was a very scary place. And you just knew that whatever happened . . . the cops weren't going to protect you. Ben was fearless. Didn't give a fuck, but . . . to my shame . . . you can't say the same about me."

A young woman from housekeeping opens the meeting

room door, starts to walk in, sees us, nods and apologizes, and walks out.

"You knew Kaylee, so you'll know what I'm saying is true," Grant says. "Other people will think it's that thing people do after someone dies where they remember them being far better than they were or forget about the ways in which they were difficult or . . . worse. But Kaylee was . . . she was . . . different. Unique. She was so sweet, so . . . genuine. She was the kindest, most caring person I've ever met. The Walshes are good people. Really good. Generous. Loving. Y'all know. But Kaylee was the best of them. The best of . . . just the best. And here's the thing . . . I couldn't admit it at the time, but . . . deep down . . . I knew she was too good for me. I think that's part of why I sabotaged it with Brandi. I don't know. That's probably a question for my therapist, but I do know this . . . She made me a better person and I've tried to honor her and do something kind for someone in her memory everyday."

"We do know first hand what you're saying is true," I say. "And we try to do the same thing."

"Probably shouldn't say this, especially on camera," Grant says, "but I'm not the same scared young man I was back then. That experience, this whole experience changed me. Altered me. I've . . . I've done things to change and better myself. I've taken self-defense training and firearms classes. I've earned a black belt in Taekwondo and a concealed carry permit. I've thought about this a lot over the years. I know it's not what Kaylee would want, but if I ever find the person who took her from us . . . from this world that needs people like her so much, well . . . let's just say have a real hard time that such a person could still be walking around freely and drawing breath and living his life after what he did."

Blade nods vigorously. "We right there with you on that. We'll have to see who gets to him first. And it's too fuckin' bad you can only kill someone like that once."

Lani says, "Are you serious? Is that what you're here to do?"

We all turn toward her.

"No," Blade says. "Of course not. And erase that part from the film. What he said and what I said." She looks over at Leaf and Book. "Not kidding. Erase it now."

49

"Are y'all really up here to kill whoever killed Kaylee?" Lani asks.

We are driving out to interview Bruce Lewis—Lani, Blade and I in our rental, Leaf and Book in theirs.

"You askin' on or off the record?" Blade says.

"Off the record," she says.

Blade smiles. "Answer the same either way. We here to investigate Kaylee's disappearance. That's all. Our job is to find out what happened. We can't do anything else. Can't make arrests. Can't prosecute. And damn sure can't execute."

"I believed you more before," she says.

I say, "Obviously, this is personal for us. Of course we can relate to the sentiments Grant expressed. All loved ones of murder victims can relate to the desire for retribution, but that's all it is—a desire, a revenge fantasy."

"I get it," she says. "I do. I've had similar thoughts and feelings, but . . . to plot and plan . . . to be here with that agenda and carry it out is . . . premeditated murder."

"And we ain't about that," Blade says. "We the good guys. We wouldn't be in business we'd be in jail if we took revenge on suspects instead of what we actually do, which is share our finding with officials."

"Of course, but this isn't like your other cases. This is so personal. Wanting to kill the person who killed Kaylee is the most natural thing in the world. But . . . wanting to and doing it are two very different things. And like I say . . . I sympathize. I'm just asking—"

"Let me give you my answer," I say. "I'm not here to commit murder. Full stop. I want justice. I want accountability. I want to expose her killer. And as much as part of me wants to . . . as much as I think he deserves to be . . . I'm not going to kill Kaylee's killer in cold blood."

"I believe you," she says.

"That mean you don't believe me?" Blade says.

"Do y'all think given the chance Grant would?"

Blade shrugs. "He ain't gonna get the chance, so . . ."

We pull into Bruce Lewis's yard to find him waiting for us.

Within a few minutes, everything is set up and we're interviewing him in his side yard in front of his truck, an old metallic blue low-slung Peterbilt truck tractor with a flat top sleeper cab, tall aluminum exhausts on either side of the cab, dual fuel tanks, and aluminum wheels.

He's standing directly in front of his rig, which means virtually all that can be seen is chrome—from the wide bumper up through the tall grille to the horns and light holders and exhaust stacks.

Both smaller and younger than I expected, he's a mid-thirties white man with somewhat of a baby face. Beneath his blue ball cap which bears the same red Peterbilt logo as the grille of the truck behind him his eyes are hidden behind dark shades.

"Everybody knows my story," he is saying. "I was coming in and saw a car on the side of the road facing the wrong way. A young woman was standing out beside it and I stopped to see if she was okay. She said she was. I asked her if she wanted to call the police. She said there was no need and that she had just called AAA. I knew it was a lie because there's no cell service along here, but I didn't call her on it. Just asked if she wanted to wait for them at our place. She said she was fine and I told her we were right over here if she needed anything."

"Was anybody with her?"

He shakes his head.

"Did it look like maybe someone could've been at some point?"

"Not sure what that means exactly, but I saw no signs of anyone else."

"Was she smoking?" I ask.

"No."

"Could you tell if she had been drinking?"

"Not that I could tell, but remember . . . I was way up in my rig and was only there a few minutes."

"Were there any other vehicles around?"

He shakes his head again. "Not a one."

"Anything suspicious at all?"

He tilts his head and looks up as if accessing his memory of that night. "No. Not really. Don't think so."

"So what'd you do next?"

"Drove over here, parked right here, and went in."

"What was she doing?"

"Every time I glanced over there she was doing the same thing—just standing there."

"Did you watch her from inside?"

"After I put my things down and washed my hands and face, I looked out the window on my door. She was still just standing there. That's when I decided I should call the cops. So I did. Looked out again a few minutes later and she was gone."

Blade says, "Was anyone at home with you?"

He shakes his head. "Just me."

"And you never saw her again?" I say.

"Never did."

"What happened next?" I ask.

"Went in and took a shower, got dressed, and started cooking dinner."

"Did you look out again or go back outside?"

"I'd look out occasionally. But when the cops showed up . . . I stopped checking."

"Which cops? Do you remember?"

"No. Well, I remember the one who came to my door later that night. Colt Stevens."

"But there was more than one at the scene?"

"Not sure."

Blade says, "Must've been 'cause you said cops."

"Maybe so. Don't know for sure."

"What about their vehicles?" I ask. "Which vehicles do you remember?"

He shrugs. "Really don't. Just not sure. But I know why you're asking. And I know who can tell you what you want to know. Let me text her to stop by. Give me just a second."

"Thanks."

When he is finished and puts his phone away, I say, "What did Stevens say when he came to your door?"

"Asked if I had seen the girl. Said she wasn't around. Told him I hadn't. He said to call them if I did. I said I would. That was it. Ate my dinner and later that night when I looked out there was nothing there—including her vehicle."

Blade says, "Did the cops ever search your house or property?"

He shakes his head. "Nope."

"Ever do any follow up at all?" I ask.

"Nope. I get calls and emails and people stopping by from time to time. Not really reporters, just like podcasters and . . . Doesn't really matter 'cause I just don't know anything. Didn't see much. Wished I'd've stayed with her until the cops came. But..."

A blue Kia Optima pulls into Lewis's driveway and a middle-aged woman with a large gardening hat gets out.

"There she is," Lewis says. "This is Ellie Auster. Ellie, these are detectives working on the Kaylee Walsh case and the film crew shooting a documentary about it. They were asking me about the police vehicles at the scene that night."

"I'm happy to tell you what I know," she says slowly with a thick Southern drawl, "but I couldn't possibly be on TV. I look a mess. Been workin' in my flowerbeds this mornin'."

Lani steps forward and says, "What if you stand there and face them and we'll just get you from the back—show off that lovely hat?"

"Sure, sweetie, I recon I could do that. Won't take but a minute to tell y'all what I know." She looks back at us, adjusting her hat with both hands. I passed by here that night. And I saw ... and I'm as certain of it as I am my own name. I saw ... Chief Alden's SUV."

"Do you remember when it was?" I ask.

"8:37 p.m. I looked at my clock because I was meeting someone at my place at nine and I wondered if I had time to stop. I didn't stop, but oh how I wish I had."

"So you passed by before I did," Lewis says. "When I came by only Kaylee's car was there."

"They always claimed Alden was never there, but I know he was," Ellie says. "Or at least his vehicle was. I didn't actually see him. Didn't see either of them. But there's no doubt in my mind —none whatsoever—that his vehicle was there."

50

"**D**o you believe her?" Lani asks.

I nod. "I do. Her and Hope. They both saw the chief's vehicle."

Lani and I have crossed the street from Bruce Lewis's place and are walking through the woods behind the spot where Kaylee crashed her car.

Leaf and Book are shooting footage and capturing sound around the crash site and Blade drove back into town.

"But," I add, "it doesn't make sense. If he was there . . . it wasn't for long."

The day is cold and the forest is sparse, its trees and understory winter-bare.

Lani says, "You think it's possible she just ran into the woods here and . . . something natural happened to her—a snake or a bear or the elements?"

I shrug. "It's possible, I guess, but this area has been searched more than any other."

"True," she says. "Did Blade say where she was going?"

I shake my head. "No."

"She left like she was on a mission," she says. "Wonder if I should've sent Leaf and Book with her to capture whatever she's doing."

"Probably best not to send them out alone with her," I say.

She smiles.

We continue on, winding through the woods along a path that provides the least resistance, passing through a small clearing, and continuing on.

"So if Alden wasn't there for long . . ." she says. "Why was he there at all?"

"If he was there early and not later," I say, "would seem that he . . . caused the accident then left the scene."

"If that's the case it doesn't getting us any closer to finding out what happened to Kaylee," she says. "Hope and Bruce both saw her after Alden was gone."

I run through the possibilities in my head.

"Here are the possibilities as I see them," I say. "Let me know what I'm leaving out. Hope and Ellie are wrong and the chief nor his vehicle where ever there. They're right and his vehicle was, but he wasn't. He was driving drunk as we know he was wont to do and he hit her, knocked her off the road and spun her around. And then after a little while he takes off. Though that doesn't explain where he and Kaylee were when Ellie came by."

"Maybe they were back here in the woods. Maybe she ran back here and he chased her. He could've given up and left and she eventually went back out to her car."

I nod. "Very possible. If he did hit her and leave . . . Colt Stevens could've cleaned everything up for him. Or . . . maybe Colt was never here. What if Alden drove his SUV somewhere to hide the damage to it and got in a patrol car and came back out to deal with Kaylee. Or maybe when Colt arrived he and Alden swapped vehicles so Alden could stay and deal with Kaylee and Colt went and hid the SUV. He could've come back out in another vehicle at which point Alden had already left with Kaylee. Colt acts as if he just got here and no ones here and he walks over and asks Bruce and Hope what they saw."

"If Alden was here or involved in any way . . . I think you covered all the options. Can't think of any others. That's impressive. You've got a good mind for this kind of work."

Eventually the sloping hill we're traversing comes to a small river, running south away from town.

"Wonder if this is one of the tributaries connected to the waterfall," she says.

"Probably," I say. "Probably connected somehow."

Her eyes widen and her mouth falls open. "What if Kaylee ran back here and fell in here. She was dazed and confused and sick and exhausted and running and falls in and drowns. And then her body was carried down stream and . . . I don't know, but maybe it wound up somewhere that was never searched. Or maybe it got trapped beneath a log or other debris or a gator got it. Are there gators around here?"

I nod slowly and think about the possibilities. "Definitely need to find out how well the river was searched and where it leads."

"It flows in the opposite direction as she was headed, as the scent the dogs tracked was, and as the sighting of her. Maybe they just didn't look in this direction as thoroughly as they should have."

"Ben will know," I say, pulling out my phone. "I'll call him and—No service. I'll call him when we get somewhere with signal. But . . . If there's still no signal in this area . . . How did Bruce text Ellie?"

"Slow that suspicious mind down just a little bit there," she says with a smile. "He was probably close enough to his house to use wifi."

51

"Yeah, Ben searched that river all the way down," Grant is saying. "It was low at the time, but we still thought it was possible she could've gone in and . . . but there was no sign of her."

Unable to get Ben on the phone, I went to Grant's room once we arrived back at the hotel.

His voice is thick with sleep, his eyes are wet and a little swimmy, and the room behind him is dark and quiet.

"Sorry if I woke you up," I say.

"No problem. Just didn't get much sleep last night."

"I'll let you go so you can get back to sleep."

"Okay, but don't hesitate to wake me up if there's anything I can do to help. And I'll be up soon. Want to help if I can."

After leaving his room, I stop by Blade's, but, like her phone, she does't answer, and I wonder what she's up to. Something she doesn't want Lani and the others to know about, no doubt.

When Lani lets me in her room, she is on the phone.

I pull out my laptop and continue to do research while I wait on her.

When she wraps up her call, she joins me on the loveseat.

"Who's your daddy?" she says.

"I actually don't know," I say.

"Me," she says. "You were supposed to say *I'm* your daddy. You know good and well when someone asks you that question what the correct answer is. And you bring in some sad shit to make me feel bad."

I smile at her. "I didn't think we were at that stage of the relationship yet, but . . . you're my daddy."

"I've arranged for the others you wanted to join us up here," she says.

"Brandi and Collins?" I ask.

She nods. "And Johnny Boy and Crystal Rose,"

"Wow. Awesome. Thank you, Daddy."

"Pleasure," she says. "And just so you know . . . I'm happy to be the daddy of this production, but if our relationship ever moves from this loveseat to the bed I want you to be the daddy."

I smile at her again and hold her gaze and something electrical passes between us.

When it becomes too much she says, "But while I'm still in daddy mode what else can I do?"

"Biggest thing at this point is identifying the Dahlonega Three. There are conflicting rumors, but we need to—"

"I'm on it," she says, and grabs her laptop off the coffee table in front of us.

"Grant said they searched the river all the way down," I say. "Even had Search and Rescue from a nearby county drag the river."

She nods. "Good to know. Everything we can take off the list, every suspect we can eliminate . . . we're getting closer and closer to closing in on the guilty party."

I nod and smile at her again. "That's exactly how this works."

"Don't act surprise that I know that," she says. "Investigative journalism isn't that much different from the kind of investigating you do."

"It wasn't surprise. It was appreciation."

"Oh."

"And I'm thinking it's time to take this relationship from the loveseat to the bed."

"Whatever you say, Daddy."

Our lovemaking is gentle and sweet, tentative at first, and eventually extremely intense. She's as responsive as any lover I've ever been with, and our various activities involve a lot of eye contact and a genuine connection.

Afterwards, we fall asleep entangled in each others arms and legs, our hot bodies beginning to cool down in the cold hotel sheets.

Evidently, we are both far more exhausted than we realize. We sleep the rest of the afternoon, and, in fact, are still sleeping that evening when Blade calls.

"Hey," I say, trying not to sound sleepy.

"Put your pants on. I need your help. And come alone."

52

I borrow Lani's rental because Blade is on ours.

When I arrive at the coordinates Blade gave me, I find an old abandoned slaughterhouse set back off an empty, rural highway.

I pull around back like she instructed me to and park next to her vehicle.

Directly in front of me are several holding pens with sections of their fencing missing. I enter there and then following through the corrals that once funneled the herd of animals, single file, to their fate. The corrals, many of which are missing several sections of panels, are designed in long, sweeping curves, presumably so that the animals couldn't see that they were being led to slaughter. The design appears to be such that they would only see the hind quarters of the poor bastard in front of them.

Part of the roof of the building has caved in and I move around it.

Obviously, the facility has been closed for quite a while, yet the stench of blood and bowels, death and decay still lingers in a surprisingly pungent way.

Eventually, I make my way to the hanging room. Beneath the hanging meat hooks that clang against each other metallically in the breeze blowing in from the opening in the roof, the concrete floor beneath is streaked black with bloodstains.

When I reach the cold storage room beyond, I find Blade standing in front of Alden Reynolds, who is strapped to a chair, a gag in his mouth held by duct tape.

Alden is slumped over, head falling forward, his hair and shirt soaked through with sweat.

Blade is holding a fifth of Jack in one hand and her phone in the other.

Looking down at her phone, she begins to read. "'Withdrawal symptoms begin within six to 24 hours of stopping or significantly decreasing heavy, long-term alcohol abuse. The symptoms can include: headache, anxiety, nervousness or irritability, insomnia, excessive sweating, upset stomach, heart palpitations, increased blood pressure and heart rate, hyperthermia, tremors, confusion, hallucinations, seizures, and delirium.' I'd say you have all of those, would you?"

He mumbles incoherently.

She glances over at me. "It's nice when they torture themselves. I've had him here since last night. Haven't laid a finger on him except to tie him up."

Once the chief law enforcement officer in town who wielded a lot of power and influence, addiction has reduced Alden to a weak, feeble, old figure.

"'Each of these symptoms can increase in intensity depending on the severity of the withdrawal,'" she continues reading from her phone. "I'd say yours is pretty severe. 'If this happens, you should go to the nearest emergency room or call 911. The severity and length of alcohol withdrawal varies based on many factors. But generally speaking, from six to 12 hours after your last alcohol-containing drink: Mild symptoms appear, like headache, mild anxiety and insomnia.

Within 24 hours of your last drink you may experience hallucinations, and your seizure risk is highest 24 to 48 hours after your last drink. Symptoms typically tend to peak between 24 to 72 hours after your last drink.' How long you think it's been? My guess is about eighteen hours. SO as bad as it is . . . it's gonna get worse. A lot worse. Or . . ." she holds up the fifth of Jack. "I can make it stop. You said earlier you were ready to talk. I hope you are. Because we're ready to hear what you have to say. And if you tell us the truth—the absolute truth and nothing else . . . I'm gonna give you this bottle and make all this go away."

She pulls out a knife from beneath her jacket, steps over to him, and slicing through one side of the duct tape from his mouth, causing the other side to dangle down, the cloth gag stuck to it.

"I . . . I . . . didn't hurt her. I swear on my life."

"Oh, that's what you doin'."

"It was an accident," he says. "Just a . . . little . . . over . . . the line. Barely touched her. Just didn't turn enough . . . and . . . a little . . . side swipe. Spun her around. She was fine. She wasn't hurt. I swear. Can I have a sip now? Just a sip."

"The whole truth and nothing but the truth first," she says.

"GIVE ME A GODDAMN DRINK," he yells. "NOW. NOW, GODDAMNIT."

"It's only gonna get worse," Blade says. "Better get it all out as fast as you can."

"I'm tellin' you . . . I swear . . . she was fine. I called Chuck."

I assume he means Chuck Finely, the officer who claimed he was driving the chief's vehicle that night.

"But . . . he was . . . couldn't . . . come . . . workin' a domestic . . . Then I heard . . . on the . . . radio . . . Colt was . . . on his way to the scene. I tol' her . . . to . . . wait . . . not say . . . anything . . . I'd . . . take care . . . her. And . . . took off. But when . . . Colt . . . she was . . . gone. I . . . swear I . . . don't . . . know where. She . . . was .

. . fine when I . . . left. That's gospel. Strap me up to . . . polygraph. I'm . . . truth. Swear."

Blade glances over at me. "You think that's the whole and nothin' but?"

I shrug. "I don't know."

"I swear. Please. Please. I . . . I'm . . . sorry I hit her, but . . . it was . . . n't . . . bad. Sorry . . . left, but . . . that . . . 's . . . all I . . . did."

"Ain't all you did even if it is," Blade says. "Chief of police drunk off his ass hits her and warns her not to say anything . . . scared her to death. No wonder she ran. No . . . fuckin' . . . wonder. But I ain't sure I believe that's all you did. Let's hear it again."

He rages again, yelling and spitting, hurling insults and profanities, but eventually tells the story again.

It's the same story.

It takes a while, but she makes him tell it a third time. And for the third time it's the same story.

By the time we're done, we both believe him.

"Whatever happened to her . . ." Blade says. "Is on you, you sad, pathetic bastard. You caused it. Whatever it was. It started with you. World would be a better place if I jammed my .45 down your throat and blew out your brain pan."

"Do it," he says. "Please. Be . . . doin' . . . me . . . favor."

"That's part of the reason why I'm not going to. But hey . . . when we drop you back off at your place . . . you feel free to do it."

53

When I get back in Lani's rental and check my phone I see I've missed several calls and texts from her.

I call her back.

"Did you get my messages?" she says.

"No. Just called you back when I saw I had missed your calls."

"Where are you?"

"Driving back into town," I say. "'Bout ten minutes away."

I had followed Blade to Alden's house and helped her deposit him there. She had given him the fifth of Jack at the conclusion of the interview and he had been compliant in a barely conscious kind of way.

"Why?" I ask. "Is everything okay?"

"We've gotten Jackson Hayes to agree to an interview tonight, but it has to be tonight. He's leaving town in the morning and won't be back for at least two weeks."

Jackson Hayes is the owner of the cabin in the woods not too far from where Kaylee vanished and has refused to grant interviews over the years.

"He's saying he's willing to give a short interview for the documentary but not be interrogated by police or private detectives. Wondered how you wanted to handle it. When I didn't hear back from you I went ahead and set up the interview. Didn't want to miss the chance of getting him on tape."

"Sorry I wasn't able to take your calls."

"I figured you and Blade were working on something you didn't want to be part of the doc."

I don't tell her just how right she is.

"How do you want to handle it?" she asks.

"What if you conduct the interview," I say. "And we give you some questions we'd like to know the answers to. See how much you can get out of him."

"I'm certainly willing," she says, "but I'd want to know what info you're looking to get out of him."

"Let me call Blade and fill her in and I'll call you right back."

I call Blade and tell her the situation and ask what she thinks about Lani doing the interview.

"Sounds like our only play. And from what I've seen of her she'll probably get more from him than we ever could." She lets out a large, long yawn. "If y'all got this, I'm gonna go back to my room and crash. Didn't sleep last night, babysitting drunk ass fuck face."

54

"Behind you is the place many believe to be where Kaylee Walsh was murdered," Lani is saying.

Appropriately, dramatically, the interview is taking place in front of what was Jackson Hayes's cabin when Kaylee vanished.

Hayes is standing beneath an oak tree in the front yard, lit with an eerie ghost-like glow, the large, nearly full moon looming just over the cabin, bathing it in a soft, pale, milky radiance.

"It unequivocally is not," Hayes says. "And I'll get into why in a moment, but . . . do you realize how many bizarre and ridiculous and even slanderous things have been said about people in this town? And one by one, over time, they've all been proven to be false. It's just . . . sad lonely people who have no life going online and coming up with crazy theories based on zero evidence because they have nothing better to do."

Lani, who is off camera, says, "But why do some rumors persist while others don't?"

"Who knows? I'm sure a psychologist or sociologist could tell you. All I know is all or nearly all of them are bonkers and can't be true. And what I know for absolute certain is that I had nothing to do with whatever happened to that poor girl. And that's the thing . . . no one knows what even happened to her. We see this all the time in every area of life. There are gaps in information and knowledge and certain humans can't accept that so they rush in to fill those gaps with absurdity because they'd rather have an untrue answer than no answer at all."

"Earlier when we spoke off camera you said you could prove you had nothing to do with Kaylee's disappearance."

"So . . . I no longer own this cabin—we'll get to that in a minute—but back when I did . . . it wasn't my primary residence. It was just a place I'd go to occasionally to get away for a few days. I wasn't here at the time Kaylee went missing. And I can prove it. I was at a LUYL in Denver."

"A LUYL?" Lani asks.

"Yes. Level Up Your Life conference. I was there all week. Not here raping and murdering a vulnerable young woman who just happened to show up at my door like a lamb to slaughter."

When he says that I can smell the old slaughter house, as if that putrid stench is trapped in my nostrils and memory.

"The police checked my alibi and it checked out," he continues. "Hundreds of people saw me."

"Did anyone else use your cabin back then?"

"No," he says, "not really."

"No or not really?"

"My nephew looked after the place for me and he may have spent the odd night here, but he wasn't here that night, and . . . the police searched the place thoroughly. And . . . if any crimes had been committed here there would be evidence and I never would've sold the place if that were the case. That's what I meant by certainty. I'm certain and have evidence to back it up —unlike all the wing nut theories out there."

"What's your nephew's name? Is he still in the area?"

"I'm not gonna say. I won't have him harassed the way I have been. I shouldn't've said anything. I wasn't thinking. It was stupid. I'd appreciate if you wouldn't include that in your film."

Once Lani finishes up with Hayes and he leaves, the new owners of the cabin, Jill and Rob Owens, come out and we have an off camera talk with them.

"We didn't want to see him," Jill is saying.

"Guy give us the creeps," Rob says.

They are a young African-American couple, handsome, athletic, intelligent, stylish.

"He comes across nice enough," Jill says, "but something . . . just isn't right."

"Nothing we can point to," Rob says, "but . . . and then when we found the blood."

"Can you tell us about that?" I say. "We heard a forensic team came in and processed the scene."

"Yeah, I should've said they found the blood. Not us. You couldn't see it, but . . ."

Jill says, "We feel so bad for Kaylee Walsh and we've had enough run-ins with some of the crazies around here . . . When a group of online citizen sleuths approached us and said they thought she could've been killed here and wanted to search the place . . . we said sure."

"They brought in cadaver dogs first," Rob says. "They alerted on a closet in the basement, so then a forensic team came in and gathered evidence. There was traces of blood in that closet. If something did happen to her here . . . that's where it was. But . . . when they had it tested they said they found traces of two humans, a male and a female, and that of a dog. And they were so combined and contaminated they couldn't use them to make a match with anyone."

"And that's a shame," Jill says, "but what the actual? Two humans and a dog? In the same basement closet. We want nothin' to do with that man or his nephew."

"Who's his nephew?" I ask.

"Cameron Cooper," Rob says.

If Lani would've had water in her mouth she'd've done a spit take. Instead she exclaims, "*The new chief of police?*"

"Yeah," Rob says. "Makes us wish we'd've never bought this place. We got it for a nice quiet get away from the city, but in some ways it seems more dangerous up here."

"Speaking of . . ." Jill says. "We're about to head back to the big bad city. We can leave y'all a key if you'd like to shoot some shots of the basement or—"

"We would love that," Lani says. "That would help us so much. We can pay you."

"Oh, no need. We're happy to help if we can."

Rob says, "Only thing we ask is you don't reveal the address or our identities."

"Absolutely. You got it. And thank you so much."

55

When we get back to the hotel we find Ben, Kay, and Scotty in the lobby.

Ben and Scotty are warm and friendly. Kay is polite but cool and stand-offish.

I had called Cameron Cooper on the way over, but he didn't answer. Which was probably best since I needed to talk to Blade first anyway. My call had been impulsive, the adrenaline from the revelation still coursing through me.

After they finish checking in, we drift over away from the front counter.

"The investigation is really going well," I say. "I think we're getting close. We've definitely uncovered quite a bit that we didn't know before. There's some critical information we need from y'all so that we can keep the momentum going. I'm sure y'all are tired, but could we meet for a little while this evening?"

Ben nods. "Of course. Why don't we do it now? Is there some place we can go?"

"We've been using the hotel conference room," Lani says. "It's right around that corner, down the hallway."

Leaf and Book walk in and Lani steps over to them, tells

them what's going on, then we all follow Lani to the conference room.

On the way, I text Blade and ask if she feels like joining us.

Inside the room, as Book and Leaf quickly set up, Lani talks to Ben, Kay, and Scotty about the approach of the documentary and reassures them that they're in good hands.

I quickly set up five folding chairs in a circle and Ben, Kay, Scotty, and I take one.

Kay appears anxious and continues to look at the door.

"The first thing I want to talk to you about is a new theory we have about a condition Kaylee possibly had," I say. "I wanted to see if any of you saw any signs or symptoms of it. We believe it was explain a lot, including the car accidents."

"Oh, my God," Ben says, "That would . . . be . . . What is it?"

"It's called Conversion disorder," I say. "We think it's possible she was suffering from it or something similar to it. It's a condition in which someone experiences physical and sensory problems, such as paralysis, numbness, blindness, deafness or seizures, with no underlying neurological explanation. There's no underlying disease or cause but the symptoms are real. It can effect a person's movement or senses—like walking, swallowing, seeing or hearing. All her friends say she didn't drink or do drugs, but she was increasingly getting into accidents."

Kay begins to cry softly.

"Did any of you notice any symptoms like these?"

"I . . ." Ben says, then seems to drift into memory.

Kay nods as she wipes her tears.

"I didn't," Scotty says, "but I was a kid."

Ben says, "The night she wrecked my car . . . She was . . . She said she had a bad headache that was affecting her vision. Said her hands weren't working right. I thought she had a migraine or maybe bumped her head in the accident. But maybe this condition could've caused the accident in the first place. Could've caused all of them."

"I had made her an appointment with our doctor," Kay says. "She had been complaining of . . . some of the symptoms you mentioned. She was supposed to come home at the end of the week and see her. She never got the chance. My poor sweet girl suffering from a condition she didn't know about. She must've been so confused and . . . scared."

"It's just a theory," I say. "There's no way for us to test it. But we do think it would explain a lot."

Kay says, "I really think . . . I think she had that . . . or at least something similar. Maybe even the early stages of MS or something."

"Thank you," Ben says. "Thanks for giving us the . . . possibility of this."

Blade opens the door and walks in.

I stand and motion her to her chair and tell her what Ben and Kay had said about Kaylee's symptoms.

"My head's hurting," Kay says, standing. "Think I'll go to the room and lie down."

"Soon as I walk in," Blade says. "You walk out."

Kay doesn't acknowledge Blade's comment nor even look in her direction.

"Closest thing to a mother I ever had," Blade says, "and you get rid of me. Okay. Fine. But then nothing—for a fuckin' decade. And now you won't even look at me. Is it guilt for dropping us off back at the pound? Is it—know what, doesn't matter what it is. I thought you were avoiding us because you didn't want to answer our questions, but you just avoiding me. Well, ignore me all you want, but I'm gonna find out what happened to the daughter you did love and then what you gonna—"

"You're the reason she went missing," Kay says, turning on Blade, fury in her face.

"*What?*" Blade's voice sounds like that of a little girl. "I had nothing to do with—"

"She called me that afternoon," Kay says. "Probably to ask for help or at least to let me know where she was going, but I missed her call. And do you know why I missed my little girl's call? Because once again I was in the principal's office with you because for the umpteenth time you had gotten in trouble. You had so much anger and meanness in you. Always gettin' into trouble and fights. And instead of taking the call that could've saved Kaylee's life . . . I was hearing how you had beaten some little boy black and blue for calling you a name or something. I couldn't even look at you after that, after your hateful, violent . . . cost me my little girl."

"We were bullied unmercifully in that school," I say. "Blade far worse than me. She wasn't mean or . . . She never started fights. And most of the time she was taking up for other kids who were being bullied, including me."

"We should've never put y'all back in foster care," Ben says. "I'm . . . so, so sorry. It's on me. But we were in crisis mode and we were up here. And I honestly believed . . . I thought it was just temporary. I thought we'd find Kaylee and bring her home, then bring y'all home."

Blade stands up. "You stay," she says to Kay. "I'm going. But I'll tell you this . . . I don't know what happened to Kaylee, but . . . And I know a lot of people think death is the worst thing that can happen to someone, but . . . you . . . What y'all put us through by putting us back in there . . . apart from dying, which puts a medical end to the suffering . . . We've been through . . ." She stops and shakes her head. "Doesn't even matter. Not like you care anyway."

Blade moves toward the door. When she reaches it, she turns around and looks at Leaf.

"Leaf," she says.

He pops up from behind the camera. "Ah, yes. Yes, ma'am."

"If the footage of that little family episode survives the night you won't."

She looks at Lani.

Lani says, "It won't. You have my word."

As Blade leaves the room, I jump up and rush out to catch up with her.

Out in the hallway I grab her and hug her, holding her tight.

"Let go of me, bitch," she says.

I don't.

She struggles to get free.

I hold her even tighter.

Eventually, she stops fighting and starts sobbing.

56

Later that night, Blade, Lani, and I are in my room, finishing up a pizza and going over the case.

Blade and I are at the small table and Lani is on the loveseat on her computer.

Going over where we are in the case will be helpful, but I'm using it as an excuse to keep Blade close.

And of course she knows.

"I know what you're doing," she says. "Ain't foolin' anybody."

I give her a quick nod of acknowledgement.

"So," I say, "we know how the accident happened, but not—"

"Wait, what?" Lani says, looking up from her laptop. "I missed something."

"This ain't for the documentary," Blade says. "Least not yet. Once we know everything, you can add it in later."

"Okay."

I say, "Alden Reynolds, driving under the influence, clipped the front quarter panel of her car and spun her around."

"And we don't get to know how y'all know that, do we?" Lani says.

"Not how we got the info, no."

She nods.

"But," I continue along my original line of thinking, "we don't know what happened after that. And we still don't know why she was up here, where she was headed."

Blade says, "Options are . . . somebody picked her up, she ran into the woods, or crossed the street to Bruce Lewis's place."

Lani says, "Sorry, I'm playing catchup here, but . . . you think Alden hit her but didn't take her or do anything to her after that?"

Blade nods.

I say, "That *is* what we believe. We believe he hit her, parked and made sure she was okay. Told her to stay put and left. He called one of his officers to help him, but he wasn't available. And Colt Stevens who wouldn't help him cover it up responds to the call, but by the time he gets there . . . she's already gone."

"If the dogs are right," Blade says, "she ran or walked for a little ways then got into a vehicle with someone."

"But we can't be sure about that."

"Blood in the basement of Hayes's cabin is suspicious."

"It is," I say, "but that cabin is a lot farther away than it seems when walkin' through the woods. Especially for someone suffering from a numerological disorder and the trauma and possible injury of a wreck."

"True."

I say, "I feel like we've learned so much, but we've still got so many huge gaping holes in the timeline and narrative."

"Mostly what we've done is eliminate shit," Blade says.

"Which is an important part of the process. I'm just ready to get on to the next part—of finding the truth of what's left."

"Oh, my . . . God," Lani says. "I think I just cracked the case."

We look over at her.

She's still looking wide-eyed at her laptop screen.

"Maybe that was an overstatement," she says, "but . . . maybe not. Maybe I should've said I may have solved where she was headed. But that might solve everything."

"Whatcha say you tell us what it is, Nancy Drew," Blade says, "and we'll—"

"Sorry. This is just . . . huge. Guess who's family has a cabin outside of Dahlonega?"

"Bitch, don't make us guess," Blade says, her voice playful but edging toward impatient frustration.

"Andrew fuckin' Collins," she says.

57

When Andrew Collins opens his hotel room door he looks startled to see us.

Blade and I are side by side and slightly behind us is Lani with a camera, capturing everything.

"What ... is ... this?" he says. "I though we were meeting in the morning."

He only checked in a couple of hours ago, but looks like he was asleep.

His thick, dirty blond hair is tousled and sticking up and his brilliant blue eyes are bloodshot and droopy.

Like the last time we saw him, he's wearing coach's shorts, but instead of a matching sports shirt and windbreaker, he has on a wrinkled t-shirt.

Blade and I push our way in. He backs up, looking confused and disoriented. Lani follows, filming.

Blade says "Your room smells like liniment and fast-food farts."

"I've got a pulled muscle and I ate drive-thru on my way up here."

I say, "Did you and Kaylee travel up here together or separately?"

"Kaylee?"

"Y'all found Kaylee? She's alive? I drove up alone. Didn't know she was—"

"Not today, dingus," Blade says. "Ten years ago."

"I don't understand."

I say, "Were you meeting at your family's cabin or did you travel together? These are not difficult questions."

"I . . . How did you—"

"Turns out skinny Moana back there on the camera is a hell of a detective," Blade says.

"Look . . . Listen . . . I had nothing to do with her disappearance. I swear. I should've said something, but I was scared. I knew people would think I did it. But I swear to you on my . . . I swear to God I didn't. I swear. I'll take a polygraph. Swear."

"Tried to scare us off down in Gainesville," Blade says. "But—"

"It was just a former student and an actor," he says. "Meant y'all no harm."

"Oh, they the ones almost got harmed," she says.

"It was stupid. I panicked. I'm sorry. But I swear I didn't have anything to do with whatever happened to Kaylee. I swear."

"Stop swearing," I say. "Makes you sound guilty as fuck. Just tell us everything. Don't hold anything back."

"Do we have to do this on camera?" he says.

"Think of it this way," Blade says. "It's more unlikely we kill you on camera."

"I . . . I was always attracted to her. She was so . . . She was . . . so sweet and beautiful. Like I said before . . . I know she was a student, but we were only a few years apart. I made overtures, but she said no. She had a boyfriend. And I never mentioned it again. I swear. But then she reaches out to me on the Saturday night before she goes missing and says . . . and asks . . . if I'm interested. Said she found out her boyfriend had been cheating on her and wanted to . . . was interested in seeing me. I told her of course I was interested. When we spoke on that Sunday . . . I suggested we get away for a few days and told her about my folks's cabin up near Dahlonega. We made plans to go later in the week and spend the following weekend, but then she said she really didn't want to wait, could I go on up sooner. I said it'd take me a day or two to square away everything and she asked if she could go on up and wait for me there. I said sure. Before I ever left Gainesville I heard she was missing. I never made it up here. I swear. I . . . I wish I would've come on up, but I didn't. I never did. I swear that's the truth. I had nothing to do with what happened to her and I have no idea what it actually was. I swear."

"What'd I tell you about that?" I say.

"Sorry, but I'm tellin' the truth."

"All this time we've been wondering what she was doing up here, where she was headed," I say. "And you've known all along."

"I was scared. And the case got so big."

"Partly because of all the unanswered questions," I say. "Like where she was headed and why."

"I know. I'm . . . a . . . I'm pathetic. So fuckin' weak. Truly. But I'm not a killer or kidnapper or whatever. There are people who can verify I was in Gainesville that whole time. I never left. I didn't come up here. I didn't hurt her or . . . anything. I just didn't."

"You didn't come and look for her?" I ask. "Didn't check your cabin to see if she was there?"

"I'm . . . sorry. I . . . know I should have. But . . . we had a security system. Still do. We're alerted every time a door or window is opened. They never were. And my little sister lived in Atlanta at the time. She used to come up and check on it and stay in it a good bit. She went to it the following week and said everything looked good. No one had been there and nothing was ... everything was fine."

"The information you had could've made a difference," I say. "Could've saved a lot of wasted time and maybe helped us find her sooner."

Blade says, "Makes me want to hurt you real bad."

When Blade turns toward Lani, Lani says, "I know I know. Consider it erased."

58

"We now think we know most everything but the final thing," I say.

It's the next morning and we're back in the hotel conference room—this time with everyone in town for the documentary.

Ben, Kay, Scotty, and Grant are at one table, across from them Brandi and Andrew Collins are at another. Across from them, Colt Stevens, in his firefighter uniform, sits alone.

Blade and I are standing between them. Lani, Leaf, and Book are to the side filming with two cameras, attempting to get the reactions.

Johnny Boy and Crystal Rose haven't shown up yet and we're doubtful they will.

"We can't be absolutely positive, but we feel relatively certain this or something pretty close to this is what happened."

The door opens and Cameron Cooper walks in.

He's in uniform without his hat.

"Sorry I'm late," he says. "Got held up at the office."

He takes a seat at the table with Colt Stevens.

"We believe Kaylee was suffering from either Conversion Disorder or something like it," I say. "It was affecting her senses and her movements, her ability to function, which led to her car accidents and other things. With the disorder symptoms can come and go and we think they did. Sometimes she seemed fine, but others she'd be unable to control her own body."

Kay, who is crying quietly, sniffles and wipes her tears.

"We believe this led to her running into Blake Christie when she dashed out for food on the Friday before she vanished. Then on that Saturday she wrecked her dad's new car. We believe both were caused by her condition."

Ben says, "Are you sure? I mean about hitting that student?"

I nod and frown. "We believe so, yes. We have a witness."

"God, I wish we had known about her condition," Ben says. "We should have. We should've realized something wasn't right with our little girl."

Kay begins crying harder and Scotty is visibly upset.

"The other thing that happened that night was she found out Grant was cheating on her," I say. "It was while she and Brandi were at the dorm party."

Everyone turns toward Grant.

It's obvious from their expressions Ben, Kay, and Scotty feel anger and betrayal.

"I wasn't cheating," Grant says. "I . . . slept with someone else. Once. It's not the same."

"That someone," I say, "was Brandi Martin."

Everyone turns from Grant to Brandi with the same shock, hurt, and anger.

"We were stupid college kids," she says. "We had been drinking and . . . I feel horrible. I'm so, so sorry. I told Kaylee how sorry I was, how it was just the one time, but . . . she was so upset, so . . . angry. The last time I ever talked to her she . . . I had just hurt her so bad."

Kay says, "She was dealing with so much . . . and we had no idea."

"She lost her best friend and boy friend in the same moment," I say. "She was already compromised and . . . and in her pain and grief she turns to one of her professors, Andrew Collins, who had made it clear that he'd like to see her socially. They make plans. His family has a cabin outside of Dahlonega. She was to go up on Monday and he would meet her later in the week when he could get free. That's why she was up here. That's where she was headed."

Everyone turns toward Collins.

Grant says, "You creepy son of a bitch. You—"

"Don't even," Collins says to him. "You're the one who cheated on her with her best friend. I never . . . touched her. Never did anything but be there for her, listen to her about what a mistake you were. I never made it up here. She vanished before I could . . . get away."

Grant looks at me. "Is that true?"

I nod. "We believe so."

"Still," Grant says to Collins, "she was your student."

"This is what we know so far," I say. "The only other thing we know . . . is that on her way to the Collins' cabin in Dahlonega, just outside of this little town of Dawson Falls . . . she was sideswiped by the drunken chief of police, Alden Reynolds."

"Really?" Coop says. "You're sure?"

I nod.

"We sure," Blade says.

"I didn't know," Stevens says. "I swear."

"Spun her vehicle around to face the wrong way on the shoulder of the highway," I say. "He turned around and pulled over to check on her. She had run into the woods when she saw him. He followed her. Ellie Auster passing by and Hope Westmacott from her kitchen window saw his vehicle there. Seeing she was okay, he told her to stay put and not say anything to anyone. As he left, he called Officer Chuck Finely to help him cover it up, but Finely was on a domestic call he couldn't get away from. In the meantime, Colt Stevens, an honorable officer, who wouldn't help Alden out of his jam, responded to the call. But by the time he got there Kaylee was gone."

"She was," Stevens says. "There was no trace of her. Her phone and purse and keys were gone and her car was locked."

"That's what we know so far," I say. "And now y'all know it. But, as I said, we don't yet know the final thing. We don't know what happened to her between the time that Alden left and Colt arrived."

Grant says, "Clearly, Collins is lying. He was with her and did something to her."

"Like you," I say, "he has an alibi. He was in Gainesville, not up here."

Colt says, "Y'all sure Alden didn't just take her."

"She was seen after his vehicle was no longer there."

Blade says, "Oh, we do know one more thing. The chief of police had a cabin in the woods not far from the crash site."

Colt looks confused and shakes his head. "He didn't. I would've—"

"Not Alden," I say. "The new chief of police. The man sitting next to you. Cameron Cooper."

Everyone turns toward Cooper.

"I . . ." he says. "I did not have a cabin up here."

"Your family did. Your Uncle, Jackson Hayes, told us you took care of the place for him, that you used it a lot."

Blade says, "Same cabin cadaver dogs alerted on and a forensic team found blood in."

He stands up suddenly, knocking his chair over in the process. "I didn't come here to play gotcha games. I wasn't anywhere near here when Kaylee went missing. I had nothing to do with her death or disappearance or whatever it was. And if that's all you got ... then you got nothin'."

He then turns and walks out.

59

"Don't appreciate being set up like that," Cameron Cooper is saying.

Blade and I are in his office. Just us. No one else. No cameras.

"It wasn't a set up," I say.

"Exactly what it felt like."

"All we did was go through everything we know so far," I say.

Blade says, "Rather than accusing us of settin' you up, why don't you tell us why you didn't mention one of the possible crime scenes was your house?"

"It's not my house," he says. "Wasn't my place. It was an old cabin my uncle had. That's it. I wasn't up here much. He paid me to check on it every now and then. I spent very little time up here. I'd check on it about once a month and I have more fingers and toes than the number of times I stayed in it over the years."

"So, why didn't you tell us about it?" she asks.

"Unlike y'all I don't want to be on TV. Don't want that kind of attention. Have no desire to become a part of this story."

"Being honest with us wouldn't've meant that you would have."

"I was in school in Atlanta at the time," he says. "I worked at night for a cleaning company. That night we're were cleaning booths at a trade show down town. I had a girlfriend. I had roommates. A boss. They'll all tell you the same thing. I was down there, not up here."

"Then who was?" I ask. "Who else had a key?"

He shrugs. "No one."

I can tell he's lying.

"Which is it?" I say. "You don't know or no one."

"I want this case solved as much as anyone," he says. "If I knew something I'd use it to close the case. I'd share the information. I would. There's just nothin' to share. That cabin is a dead end. Just like all the others in this case."

"How long after that night before you went back to the cabin?" I ask.

"Two weeks . . . maybe. Round there."

"And what did you find?"

"Nothin'."

"Nothing was different since the last time you had been in it?"

"I'm not sayin' that. Think the maid and the maintenance man had been in since I was —"

"What you're sayin' is it had been cleaned," I say. "And some repairs done."

"Nothin' suspicious about that. It was cleaned at least once every two weeks if no one was using it—more often if it was being used. Uncle Jax used to rent it out some. The maid would clean it and if she saw anything that needed repairing or if I did or if Uncle Jax just had something he wanted done, the handyman would do them."

"And what had he repaired?" I ask.

He shakes his head slowly and frowns. "Don't start readin'

shit into this. I already know y'all are gonna lose your minds. A leak in the basement."

"In the basement closet where the blood was found?" I ask.

"I don't know anything about any blood bein' found in there," he says.

"Who you covering for?" Blade asks.

"I'm not. I know y'all want to solve this case. And I want you to. Hell, I want to, but this is a dead end."

"We gonna find out," Blade says.

"There's nothin' to find out."

"Did you interview the Dahlonega Three?" I ask.

"That's another dead end. I understand, but you're grasping at—"

"Are they who you're covering for?"

His left eye twitches—a tell to let us know something has landed.

"Did they have a key to the cabin?"

"I've got to do some actual police work," he says, standing up, "so if y'all will excuse me."

60

When we get back to the hotel, we find Lani, Grant, and Scotty in the conference room.

"Where are we with the Dahlonega Three?" I ask Lani.

Before she can respond, I notice Grant's cheek is red and his left eye is swollen.

"What happened to you?" I ask.

"Got into it with Collins," he says. "He's stronger and faster than he looks."

Blade says, "That's why you always carry a weapon."

"I do, but . . . just wanted to kick his ass, not kill him," he says.

Scotty stands up. "Dad and I are about to go search the woods again. He wants to and I don't want him out there alone. Seems futile but it gives him something to do."

"Be careful."

"Oh, and by the way," he says, "Brandi left. Said she didn't come up here to be humiliated."

Grant says, "I'll be shocked if Collins doesn't leave too."

"I'll check in with y'all when we get back," Scotty says, then walks out, closing the door behind him.

"I talked to one of them," Grant says.

"One of who?" I ask.

"The Dahlonega Three," he says. "When we were up here searching that first week after Kaylee disappeared. Didn't know he was one of the three at the time, but . . ."

"When and where was this?" I ask.

"The first day while we were searching," he says. "I was searching for her. I had just come out of the woods on a dirt road not far from some cabins. He was checking one of the mailboxes on the side of the road."

"I've got about all there is to get on the three of them," Lani says. "And I'm willing to trade."

"Sexual favors? 'Cause I'm sure you thinkin' of him," Blade says, nodding toward me, but . . . my dance card is embarrassingly empty at the moment, so if you wanna give it a go . . ."

"The you-show-me-yours-I-show-you-mine I was thinking about was what you learned from Cooper."

"Just that he coverin' for someone," Blade says. "And an even stronger belief that Kaylee was killed in that cabin."

"The Dahlonega Three as they have come to be known . . ." Lani says. "Ryan Holloway, Dallas Henry, and Trevor Hitchens. Hitchens is dead. Henry is in prison. And Holloway is a minister."

Blade says, "So it's more like the Dahlonega One-and-a-half. And it's about to be less than that. Jus too bad one of 'em already dead."

"Remember the gas station we stopped at on the way into town the first night?" Lani says. "The one in prison . . . Dallas Henry . . . he's the son of the man who owns it. And the one who's dead, Trevor Hitchens . . . he belonged to Rick Hitchens, the guy who approached us on the sidewalk and has been making all the jokes over the years about having Kaylee tied up in his basement."

"Any of them have a connection to Cameron Cooper?"

"Not that I've found," she says, "but I'll keep looking."

"I have a rapport with Ryan—the one that became a minister," Grant say. "We're Facebook friends and have messaged here and there over the years. Now I'm wonderin' if he . . . You think he checks in occasionally to see what we know?"

Lani says, "If he had something to do with it he may very well be."

"Could've gone into the ministry to make up for what he did," I say.

"That's what he gets in touch to do—ask about updates," Grant says. "I mentioned the documentary to him and he asked a lot of questions. Said let him know if he could help with anything and said we should get together while I'm in town."

Blade says, "And you surely should. As soon as possible. See if he's available tonight."

61

"I have nothing to hide and I want to come clean," Ryan Holloway is saying.

We are in our rental, he, Grant, and Blade in the backseat, me and Lani in the front. Lani is turned around in the passenger seat, a camera on her shoulder, capturing everything Reverend Ryan says.

He's an early-thirties white man with a smooth, youthful face, blue eyes, blondish hair, a calm demeanor, and a soft voice. He's wearing a black suit that fits him nicely and, though he's neither Catholic nor Episcopal, a clerical collar. Like his suit, his shoes are expensive, and like his diamond encrusted rings, his puffy, quaffed, blown-back hair, makes him look more like a televangelist than a small-town pastor.

"We were kids back then, barely out of our teens," he says, "and though I did a few foolish things, I never hurt anyone, and the only illegal thing I ever did was speeding and underage drinking. That was back before I was saved and accepted God's call on my life."

"Clearly you a new man," Blade says.

"I am. Oh, I know you're mockin' me, but I don't mind."

I pull out of the parking lot of his church and onto the road.

"Take us through it," I say.

"We were on our way to a party at the old Hayes cabin," he says. "Driving along here. We were supposed to be going to work, but we had decided to blow it off and have a party instead."

We drive the route the three young men took to work that night, passing the gas station we stopped at when we first got to town.

"The three of us worked together," he says, "but we weren't close. Trevor and Dallas were somewhat close to each other, but none of us were best friends or anything."

"Help-hide-a-body close?" Blade asks.

He shakes his head.

"I want y'all to know—y'all may already, but I have a TV ministry on the Eternal Word Network. In an upcoming show I'll be sharing my involvement in the events of that night and the impact they had on me."

"Why now?" I ask.

"In conjunction with the tenth anniversary. It'll dovetail nicely with this documentary. I'd appreciate it if you'd mention my show and the fact that our church is going to have a prayer vigil the night of the tenth anniversary. We're going to pray without ceasing for ten hours on the tenth year and expect God to bless us tenfold."

"But why are you sharing your story at all now?" I ask. "Why'd it take so long? And why not go to the police?"

"I did."

"You've talked to the police?"

"Yes, the chief is my cousin. I spoke to him—well, to be honest . . . It has been within the last few years. If I'm . . . The only thing I regret is not sharing my story sooner, but . . . I did speak with the GBI back when it first happened. All three of us did, but . . . we were less than forthcoming. And then later when I received my calling and . . . I wanted to share it, but it's not just my story, and I didn't feel at liberty to discuss it until . . . Well, after Dallas went to prison and Trevor went home to be with the Lord."

Blade says, "You were afraid of them."

"God has not given us a spirit of fear, but—"

"But you were scared."

"I wanted to be prudent and wise—wise as serpents and innocent as doves."

"What is Henry in prison for?"

"Drugs, weapons, and . . . murder."

"We're coming up on the crash site," I say.

He leans up in his seat and looks out the front window. "We were just riding along and we see her car and about a hundred yards down the way we see her. She held her thumb out and Dallas told Trevor to stop the car. We pulled over and she got into the backseat with me. She was so pretty. And nice. Very sweet. But I thought I could—she seemed a little shaken up from the accident. We asked her what happened and she said the car just got away from her. We asked where she wanted to go and she said just away. Said she'd come back for the car later. Dallas told her we were goin' to a party and asked if she wanted to come."

"What did she say?"

"She never really answered that I recall."

"Who was throwing the party?"

"I mean . . . I guess we were, but it was more like . . . we'd all just get together sometimes. I think it was Dallas who had the idea."

"Why the Hayes cabin?"

"I had a key. We'd use it sometimes."

"Why'd you have a key?"

"The cabin belonged to Cameron's uncle on his dad's side. He gave me a key to check on it and clean it when he couldn't make it up to do it. He lived in Atlanta at the time. We never did . . .we meant to call into work and let them know we weren't coming in that night, but we never did."

I take the next right and drive toward the cabin.

"She asked us for a ride," he says. "We had no idea what was going on. And really at that point nothing was going on. She just wanted to get away from her car. We all got it. We didn't—"

"She was sick," I say. "And traumatized from being in a wreck. She had hit her head. She was dazed."

"We didn't know any of that," he says.

Blade says, "Thought you were a man of God who had nothing to hide and wanted to come clean. Y'all knew good and goddamn well she was out of it and that's just how y'all wanted her."

"We weren't like that," he says. "I wasn't like that. I guess I thought she had been drinking. We were kids. And if you use God's name in vain again I'll terminate this interview."

"Y'all kill me with that shit," she says. "We're talkin' about you and your rapist, murdering buddies picking up a vulnerable girl to take her to take advantage of her . . . and you gonna get high and mighty about the language I use."

"I swear to Almighty God it wasn't like that . . . or I didn't think so at the time. It wasn't for me. Maybe I was naive. But I swear to you I'm tellin' the truth."

We pull up to the cabin and get out.

"Are we going in?" he asks.

"You bet your sweet holy ass we are," Blade says.

"I just thought we were going to ride the route we took that night."

"House hold bad memories for you?" I say. "Don't want to go back in?"

"Not for . . . me. I'm tellin' you I didn't do anything."

"Then tell us who did," I say. "Was the party in the basement?"

"No, why do you ask that? It was just in the . . . It was sort of everywhere. All around."

Blade unlocks the front door and pushes it open. Feeling on the wall inside, she turns on the entryway light.

"How many people showed up for it?" I ask.

From the far edge of the tree line, Ben and Scotty step out of the woods. When they see us, they wave and start to walk over.

"How many people?"

"Not too many. Less than fifteen. Guys and girls. That's the thing . . . if Trevor or Dallas had any intention of doing anything to her they wouldn't've thrown a party and invited a bunch of people."

"We only have your word for it that they did," Blade says.

"It's the truth. They weren't bad guys. They wouldn't hurt anyone. Wouldn't take advantage of someone. They just wouldn't. It was just a typical teenage party. We didn't want to go to work anyway and when a pretty girl wanted to hang out with us . . ."

As Ben and Scotty walk up, Ben says, "We walked all the way through the woods from the crash site. It took a long time and was very difficult. I don't think . . . in her condition . . . Kaylee could do it."

"She didn't," Blade says.

"She got a ride over here," I say, nodding toward Ryan. "Reverend Ryan here and two of his friends picked her up on the highway and drove her over here."

Ben looks at Ryan with a mixture of shock and anger. "You did? Why?"

"'Course he wasn't a reverend back then," Blade says.

"It was just a party. She came with us."

"He's taking us through what happened that night," I say. Then to Ryan add, "Lead the way."

He slowly, reluctantly steps over and enters the cabin.

We follow. Blade and me, then Lani with the camera, followed by Grant, Ben and Scotty.

Ryan turns on the lights and looks around.

"It's different now. Nicer. But the layout is the same. We had booze on the—there wasn't an island back then, just a kitchen table. We had the booze on it. The one rule we had was no smoking inside the cabin, so there was a steady stream of smokers going back and forth outside. Some of the time we played music on an old stereo system and some of the time a guy named Goon played an acoustic guitar. It was very chill. Just young people hanging out. The . . . there was a different couch, an old one with a slip cover on it, and it was in a different place—over there on that wall. I remember there was a new couple. They were on the couch making out most of the night. They disappeared into the guest bedroom for a while at some point, but otherwise were on that couch."

"What was Kaylee doing?" I ask.

"There was an old recliner in that corner over there. For a while she just sat there and seemed to be taking it all in. She'd . . . close her eyes a lot like she was just enjoying the music."

"She was concussed," Blade says. "She was probably going in and out of consciousness."

"I . . . I didn't think so at the time. How would we know if she—"

"You picked her up from a wreck," Grant says. "Y'all couldn't've been that obtuse."

"I'm sorry. We just didn't know. I never would've . . . She seemed fine. I would've taken her to the hospital if I had known . . . Or called an ambulance. But she seemed fine. Just sleepy."

Ben says, "My poor little girl was . . . she wasn't well . . . may have been bleeding internally . . . and y'all were dancing and drinking and . . . while she sat there . . . dying."

"I'm tellin' you . . . she was fine. Like I say . . . maybe a little tired and sleepy, but probably just enjoying the vibe. She seemed happy to be here. Very peaceful. I do not lie. I'm telling you the whole truth."

"What happened next?" I ask.

"There was a girl I was interested in. Ashley. She showed up late. When she went out to smoke I went with her. When I came back in . . . I was focused on Ashley. So I'm not sure how long it was, but at a certain point . . . I realized Kaylee wasn't in the recliner. I looked around and didn't see her. I asked where she was and no one knew. It upset Ashley, but I started looking for her—for Kaylee. I searched the entire house. Eventually found her on the pullout couch in the basement. I asked if she was okay. She said she was . . . that she was just tired. She asked if she could sleep for a little while. I said sure."

"Was anyone down there with her?" I ask.

"No. Absolutely not. I swear. I would've never left her with someone. I told her I'd check on her in a little while. When I got back up here Ashley was talkin' to another guy, giving me the cold shoulder."

"Oh, you poor thing," Grant says.

"I'm just sayin' . . . I did the right thing. I'm tellin' the truth about everything that happened. I kept an eye on that door." He nods toward the basement door. "No one went down there. A little later I took her some water. She drank a little and said she didn't know why she was so sleepy. I told her to . . . I asked her if she wanted me to call anyone for her and she said no. I told her to rest and I'd be back a little later. Later, as the party was winding down . . . I went back down to let her know. She said she was so sleepy and didn't have anywhere to go. She asked if she could sleep there that night and she'd have a ride the next morning. I told her sure, no problem. I wrote my name and number on a piece of paper and left it and the glass of water on the table beside her."

"And you left her here alone," I say.

"I thought I was doing a good deed," he says. "If Cameron's

Uncle Jackson found out I'd be in trouble. This was a rental. I just let her stay for free. It wasn't the first time I had done that. I thought I was doing—"

"A good deed," Grant says. "We know."

"I came back the next day to clean up from the party and check on her," Ryan says. "I worked at night and slept during the day, so it was . . . I slept later than I meant to, so it was nearly night when I got back here. I wasn't expecting her to be here by then anyway. And she wasn't. But . . . the closet door was open and the carpet had been pulled up. That was it. There was no blood or anything. No signs of violence. Just the carpet was missing and the bare foundation was a little wet. I didn't know what to do. I cleaned everything. And I told Cameron there had been a leak. He told me he'd call the maintenance man and let me know when to meet him to let him in. That was it. I swear before God. That's the truth. I honestly, truly believed she had gotten sick and threw up in the closet or got confused. Thought it was the bathroom or something. I didn't know. But it never crossed my mind that anything could be seriously wrong."

"He's tellin' the truth."

We turn to see Cameron Cooper walking in the room.

He's not in uniform, but his firearm is in his hand instead of the holster clipped to is jeans.

"Bullshit," Grant says.

"Interview is over," Cooper says. "Come on, Ryan. You're coming with me."

"I have nothing to hide," Ryan says. "My conscience is clean. God knows my heart."

"I know that," Cooper says, "but their's aren't. They're looking for someone to blame for—"

"We're looking for the truth," I say.

"Well, he's given y'all that, so . . ."

"Why is your gun drawn?" I say.

"Ryan is a pure soul," he says. "Always has been. He's innocent of . . . All he did was help a young woman in need and—"

"And it led to her death," Blade says.

"Nothin' he did. That's not on him. Good Samaritan Law protects him from—"

"If he didn't kill her he knows who did," Blade says.

"He doesn't and neither do I. If I did . . . I'd arrest them."

"Was it Dallas or Trevor?" I ask Ryan. "Or someone else who was at the party? Or did you come back and find her dead and panic and hide her body?"

"I didn't. That's not what happened. I swear before God. I wish I knew what happened, but I just don't."

"We're leaving," Cooper says. "Now."

Grant steps up behind Ryan wraps his arm around his throat and presses what looks to be a .38 revolver to his temple. "Not goin' anywhere 'til he admits what he did."

Cooper raises his weapon and takes aim at Grant.

Ryan holds his arms out more than up, as if striking a crucifixion instead of surrender pose. "The Lord is my shepherd," he whispers. "I shall not want. He maketh me to lie down in green pastures. He leadeth me beside still waters."

Cooper says, "Drop it. Right now. Or you're dead."

"You have to hit him to hit me," Grant says. "All I want to know is what he did and where she's buried."

Ryan continues to murmur quietly. "He restoreth my soul. He leadeth me in the paths of righteousness for his name's sake."

"I'm a hell of a shot," Cooper says. "I've been trained. I can take you out. Tell him."

"Put your gun down," Grant says.

Without taking his eyes off Grant, Cooper tilts his mouth toward us. "Y'all better tell him to drop it or he's dead."

"Yea, though I walk through the valley of the shadow of

death," Ryan whispers, "I will fear no evil: for thou art with me; thy rod and thy staff they comfort me."

"You the one walked in here with your gun drawn," Blade says.

"I'm the chief of police," he says.

"Off duty," Grant says.

"I'm never off duty. Not ever."

"Why're you doin' this?" I ask Cooper.

"I told y'all. I have to look out for him. Promised my mom I would. He's too naive and trusting for—"

"He killed Kaylee," Grant says.

"No, he didn't," Cooper says.

"Thou preparest a table before me in the presence of mine enemies. Thou anointest my head with oil; my cup runneth over."

"Okay," Cooper says. "Times up. Drop the weapon or die."

Blade draws her weapon and points it at Cooper. "Let's slow down on threatenin' to kill people," she says.

"You stupid . . . You just pulled a weapon on a police officer."

"I pulled a gun on an unhinged cousin tryin' to protect his family member. You came in here with your gun out. You started all this."

Ben says, "Grant, why are you doing this? Put the gun down. This is not the way."

"No. This is all his fault."

"What is?"

"Everything. All of it. He can't get away with it. He just can't."

"This isn't the way. Please. He tried to help her. He—"

"No. He killed her."

"I don't think he did. But even if he did . . . this isn't the way."

"He got her killed."

"Surely goodness and mercy shall follow me all the days of my life, and I will dwell in the house of the Lord for ever."

I think about what Grant said—*He got her killed*—and remember where he said he saw him, over here close to the cabin.

Ben must be having similar thoughts because he says, "Grant, didn't you say you walked all the way through the woods that first day we were searching up here. When we split up. I went south, following the river, but you came north—in this direction. Did you not come out where we did? Near the cabin. And you were so late getting back to the hotel that night. I thought you were out here searching that whole time because you . . ."

Everyone but Blade turns toward Grant.

"That's right," Scotty says. "You told me you . . . You said you saw this cabin. Didn't . . . Wasn't significant back then, but now . . ."

"Grant," Ben says. "Did you find Kaylee? Did you have something to do with . . . her . . ."

"What?" Grant says. "No. Absolutely not. I . . . would never hurt her. I would never do that to her."

His protestations are weak and unconvincing.

Of course it was someone close to her and not a stranger, an ex-boyfriend and not an opportunistic or serial killer. Of course all the wild theories and conspiracies were wrong.

"Do what to her?" I ask.

"Kill . . . Whatever was done to her. I'm not . . . That's not me. Not who I am. It's all because of what he did."

"Put the gun down," I say to Grant. "Tell us what happened."

"If . . . he hadn't done what he did . . ." Grant says, nodding toward Ryan.

"Grant," Ben says. "What did you do?"

"Nothing," he says, his voice cracking a little. "Didn't . . .

mean to . . . do anything. None of this would've happened if he hadn't brought her here. And if Collins hadn't taken advantage of her—a student."

"She'd never've turned to him if you hadn't cheated on her," Blade says.

She now has her weapon pointed at Grant.

"I loved her so much," he says. "Was the only one who did. Not all the others. Not this guy. Not Collins. I . . . But I was young and stupid and I . . . fucked it up."

"Just tell us what happened?" I say.

"I thought she was . . . I thought . . . they were . . . It was . . . You could tell there had been a party and she was . . . She looked hung over and like she had been . . . I thought she had . . . The whole place reeked of pot and sex. I thought she was . . . I just lost it. I didn't mean to . . . I've tried to make up for it every day of my life. I'm sorry. I'm so sorry."

He shoves Ryan forward, puts the gun to his own forehead and pulls the trigger.

The explosion is deafening in the small space and my ears begin to ring.

62

Three days later, after an extensive search of the property, Kaylee's remains were found in an old, abandoned well near the tree line on the back left corner of the lot.

We now know most of what happened to her and why. We can now bring her home and bury her. But I can find no comfort in any of it.

"Thought I'd feel . . . something," Blade says.

"Me too."

We're standing not far from the back of the cabin watching as forensic techs are removing Kaylee's bones from the well.

Out of respect, Lani has pulled the crew and we are the only ones present besides those doing the unthinkable work.

"Feel emptier now," I say.

"Didn't even get to take from him what he took from her," she says, and I know all along she wanted to be the one to spring Kaylee's killer's mortal coil. "He robbed us of that."

We are quiet a moment, watching, witnessing.

"Think about all we been through," Blade says. "This is the . . . most . . . hollowed out . . . I ever felt."

"Finding her . . . finding her killer . . . figuring out what happened and why . . . has driven us for so long. Now . . . it's gone."

"I—"

Ben, Kay, and Scotty walk around the corner of the house and over to where we are.

Silently, tearfully, we all direct our attention toward the strangers handing all that remains of the sweetest, kindest, most positive person any of us ever knew.

"Y'all gave us our little girl back," Ben says. "Answered the questions that have tormented us for so long. Given us the chance to bring her home where she belongs. We can never . . ." he breaks down and begins to cry harder, silent tears turning to sobs.

"We can never thank you enough," Kay says. "Anymore than we can ever apologize enough for what we did—for what I did. For the grudge I've held. I'm so . . . so . . ." She steps over and pulls me and Blade into a hug.

At first Blade remains rigid, resisting this thing she's most wanted for so long.

"Please . . ." Kay says, " . . . forgive . . . me."

Blade unclenches and leans in, giving herself over to the hug and to the closest thing to a mother she's ever had.

Before long, Ben and Scotty have joined us in a broken family embrace, and for a fleeting . . . bittersweet moment, I feel Kaylee's presence with us, and I'm shattered in a way I never knew possible.

63

"Where we go from here?" Blade says.

I know how she feels, why she's asking. So much of our lives have been building to this and now it's over.

I feel lost, adrift, like something is missing.

We've had this driving purpose present in everything we've done for so long and now it's gone. Can't help but wonder if this is what retirement feels like.

"Good question," I say.

Blade, Lani, and I are in our rental car. We are driving home, so I take her question to be more existential than literal—or at least related to our work.

"I'm headed home to hug Alana and spend time with her," I say, "but I assume you mean in a more spiritual sense."

"*Spiritual?*" Blade says. "I damn sure didn't mean it like that. I mean . . . You know what I meant."

"What about searching for your parents?" Lani says.

"*Fuck, no,*" Blade says.

I shrug.

Blade jerks her head over at me. "You actually considerin' that shit?"

I shrug again. "I don't know."

"Nothin' but more pain down that path," she says.

"Maybe," I say. "Probably, but . . . what we just experienced with the Walshes . . . I don't know. I might be . . ."

"What about spending more time with the Walshes?" Lani says. "Repairing that relationship. Seems like there's a real opening there."

I nod. "I can see that being a possibility."

"I meant for work," Blade says. "What we gonna do now that we . . ."

"Y'all could always investigate who killed my mom," she says. "Karen's been wanting to do a documentary about it."

I look over at her. "Is that something you'd like us to do?"

She nods. "I would."

"Well, look at that," Blade says. "Seems we already know where we goin' from here. And . . . with TV money to get us there."

UNTITLED

Gone in the Night by Michael Lister

ABOUT THE AUTHOR

New York Times bestselling and award-winning novelist Michael Lister is a native Floridian best known for his acclaimed John Jordan "Blood" mystery thriller series.

Michael grew up in north Florida near the Gulf of Mexico and the Apalachicola River in a small town world famous for tupelo honey.

Captivated by story since childhood, Michael has a love for language and narrative inspired by the Southern storytelling tradition.

Before becoming a full-time novelist in 2000, Michael taught high school, worked as a college professor and inspirational speaker, owned and operated a bookstore, wrote a popular syndicated column, served as a newspaper editor, operated a community theater, wrote plays and screenplays, and worked for a production company. He has lectured extensively in the areas of creative writing, film, literature, spirituality, and self-help.

In the 90s, Michael was the youngest chaplain within the Florida Department of Corrections. For nearly a decade, he served as a contract, staff, then senior chaplain at three different facilities in the Panhandle of Florida—a singular experience that led to his first novel, 1997's critically acclaimed, **POWER IN THE BLOOD**.

Michael is also the author of the Burke and Blade Panama City Beach PI series (**THE NIGHT OF, etc.**), the 1940s Jimmy Riley noir series (**THE BIG GOODBYE, etc.**), and the thrillers

DOUBLE EXPOSURE, BURNT OFFERINGS, and **SEPARATION ANXIETY.**

Michael is the recipient of two Florida Book Awards—for **DOUBLE EXPOSURE** and **BLOOD SACRIFICE**, respectively. His work has spent time on both the *New York Times* and the *USA Today* Bestseller lists, been translated into German, and adapted into stage plays. Currently, **DOUBLE EXPOSURE** is in development for a feature film and the John Jordan books for a TV series.

Michael lives in his beloved North Florida, where in between writing stints, he enjoys time with his family and friends, playing basketball, and making music.

ALSO BY MICHAEL LISTER

Books by Michael Lister

(John Jordan Novels)

Power in the Blood

Blood of the Lamb

Flesh and Blood

(Special Introduction by Margaret Coel)

The Body and the Blood

Double Exposure

Blood Sacrifice

Rivers to Blood

Burnt Offerings

Innocent Blood

(Special Introduction by Michael Connelly)

Separation Anxiety

Blood Money

Blood Moon

Thunder Beach

Blood Cries

A Certain Retribution

Blood Oath

Blood Work

Cold Blood

Blood Betrayal

Blood Shot

Blood Ties

Blood Stone

Blood Trail

Bloodshed

Blue Blood

And the Sea Became Blood

The Blood-Dimmed Tide

Blood and Sand

A John Jordan Christmas

Blood Lure

Blood Pathogen

Beneath a Blood-Red Sky

Out for Blood

What Child is This?

(Jimmy Riley Novels)

The Big Goodbye

The Big Beyond

The Big Hello

The Big Bout

The Big Blast

(Merrick McKnight / Reggie Summers Novels)

Thunder Beach

A Certain Retribution

Blood Oath

Blood Shot

(Remington James Novels)

Double Exposure

(includes intro by Michael Connelly)

Separation Anxiety

Blood Shot

(Sam Michaels / Daniel Davis Novels)

Burnt Offerings

Blood Oath

Cold Blood

Blood Shot

(Love Stories)

Carrie's Gift

(Short Story Collections)

North Florida Noir

Florida Heat Wave

Delta Blues

Another Quiet Night in Desperation

(The Meaning Series)

Meaning Every Moment

The Meaning of Life in Movies

MORE: Do More of What Matters Most and Discover the Life of Your Dreams

Printed in Great Britain
by Amazon